The Man Who Had Everything

THE MAN WHO HAD EVERYTHING

BY

LOUIS BROMFIELD

PUBLISHED BY

P. F. Collier & Son Corporation

NEW YORK

A short version under the title of
"The Three Faces in the Mirror"
appeared in one magazine installment.

The Man Who Had Everything

Part One

Part One

QUITE SUDDENLY IN THE VERY MIDST OF THE
party, he saw the house again, gray and old and
covered here and there with the patine of golden
lichen, its ancient tiled roof spotted with little
clusters of monkspurse, which were bright yellow in June and now in October had turned
miraculously to silver. It was there very clearly
before his eyes, in spite of the noise and heat

[3]

of the long room and in spite of the muted mathematical music of the two hot piano-players. He saw the garden running down to the river bordered with wild flags and mottled plane trees, and the marshes beyond with the little belvedere on its island white against the pale gray and gold of the beach forest. It was all still and green and damp and dappled with the pale champagne sunlight of late October, just as he had seen it for the first time as he opened his eyes and looked out of the window where the tortoise-shell cat lay sleeping on the sill. And he felt the same faint shock of surprise that the country was still so green in northern France in late October when in Illinois it would have been a cacophony of purple and red and gold. The air was soft and sleepy instead of being clear and hard. There was a whole range of green from paleness of the marsh grass to the deep green-blue of the iris leaves by the edge of the river. The plane trees had turned biscuit colored and a few crisp

[4]

fallen leaves lay scattered over the grass and along the edges of the gravel path leading down to the little bridge.

Without thinking he reached up and touched the scar on the side of his head and then all at once he was back at the party again and Jimmy Beaumont was seated beside him and talking, with a glass of champagne in one hand and a half-smoked cigar hanging from the corner of his plump, sensuous mouth. The cigar fascinated him. He had never seen Jimmy without it, even when he had called in the early morning at Jimmy's flat to find him still in bed, half buried beneath a clutter of newspapers and torn envelopes, with a breakfast tray balanced on his little round stomach. For a moment it occurred to him that perhaps it was always the same cigar, an indestructible cigar which went on and on, burning and smoking, yet eternal. He wondered whether Jimmy removed it even when he made love. For Jimmy he had a deep affection, forged in fires of a long and stormy

[5]

association. Jimmy rarely kept his word; he would cheat his own mother quite blandly. He would steal your girl if he could. Yet there was something about him, a recklessness, an unmorality, an unscrupulousness, which never failed to fill Tom with envy. Jimmy had such a good time out of life and no one ever held anything against him. He was, thought Tom, a dissipated, middle-aged cupid, with a garish twist which made him irresistible. Even in his white tie and tail coat he seemed to be wearing a red necktie and a checkered waistcoat. It was impossible to destroy his quality even at a swell party, perhaps because Jimmy was impressed by nothing in life save talent and approached everything with his tongue in his cheek.

"Well, you can't kick," he was saying. "You've thrown a party that's the top. Look at Fanny."

Fanny stood in a corner by the piano, giving an imitation of Mrs. Harding planting a memorial tree, while the two hot piano-players softly

played "Columbia, the Gem of the Ocean."
Fanny was over seventy and played Maisie's
mother in the play, but at the moment she was
showing all the vitality of a woman a third her
age. Part of it was champagne, but most of it
was Fanny herself. There was a little circle
about her, laughing and drinking. It was vitality, thought Tom, which lay at the root of all
charm—a vitality like old Fanny's off which
other less fortunate people fed perpetually.
"People," he thought, "whole audiences have
been feeding off Fanny's vitality for years;
they've been feeding off me, too."

It was a party to celebrate his thirty-seventh
birthday and the last night of a play, his own
play, which had run for three hundred and two
performances. The room was filled with people,
drinking champagne, eating sandwiches of pâté
de foie gras, making wise-cracks and small
bitcheries. It was a roomful of wit and intelligence, of malice and disillusionment, and all
the people in it talked the way all the people

he knew always talked. They were the clever ones, and they knew it. They were the successful ones, and they knew that, too, so there was in everything they said and did an arrogant carelessness. Nowhere in the world were there more clever people gathered together in the same room. And the room was like them and set them off as the proper frame adds something subtle and important to a picture.

It was a long narrow room with walls of Veronese green, and extravagant curtains of stiff white material at the windows at both ends. Above the low furniture hung the very pictures which belonged in such a room—a harsh Picasso, two Vlamincks full of vigor and unadulterated white, a Segonzac, a Moorish Matisse full of poison greens and candy pinks, and a lot of Derain black-and-whites. There were a brilliance and a hardness about the room which gave him satisfaction. After all, it was much more his creation than Sally's. Houses did not much interest her, even her own, and so she

[8]

had left it all to him. It was much more his room than hers. If she had done it, it would have been frivolous and gay and rather hysterical and silly, and it would have suited her, perhaps, but made a poor background for all the people who were here tonight, the lawyers and actors, the editors and politicians, the playwrights and novelists, the singers and dancers, the women who were beautiful and the women who were fashionable. All of them were there because they were the successful ones. That was why they had come together, admiring yet envious of one another, pleased and yet bitter with the subtle gall of a bitterness which was at the same time frustration. They were the fortunate and the unscrupulous and their glitter was a trifle inhuman.

For the first time, perhaps because he was tired and a little bored, he looked at the room with detachment, and saw that it was very like what he had dreamed of long ago as a boy. It was indeed more than that, more precise and real than anything he had dreamed, because out of ignorance he had dreamed vaguely, and all this about him was definite and clearly cut. It was a kind of apotheosis of modernity and of America and of New York. And it was all his, this big, handsome, expensive room in which there was no one person who was a failure or even mediocre. All this music and caviar and champagne was his and he had made it himself.

"So what?" he thought.

Fanny had finished her imitations in the corner and the two hot piano-players were resting, one of them, a dark Jewish boy with a long nose, was wiping the palms of his hands with his handkerchief, and the other one, half turned away from the piano, was talking to Maisie. It struck him suddenly that Maisie looked dazzling tonight. Then from belowstairs the Viennese band took up the task of keeping the hot smoky air filled with music. Softly at first, and then more and more clearly, the delicious sounds of

"Frühlingstimmen" rose up the winding staircase from the hall below. It was a good idea, the two kinds of music, the pianos, disillusioned, hard, playing jazz with a clean Bach-like precision, and the orchestra belowstairs, sentimental, swooning, and romantic. Listening to it, he was aware, as he always was in the presence of such waltzes, that life was not good enough and that love was a poor, sordid affair, baffling and unsatisfactory in contrast to the intimations of such music. That, he supposed was the appeal of Viennese waltzes. Perhaps if one made love to Strauss waltzes, love would cease to be the poor, shabby, physical thing it had come to be and attain once more that quality of Paradise which he had known long ago. There were women in the room he had lived with and others who at times stirred his desire, but with none of them, except perhaps for a moment or two with Maisie, had he found anything but boredom and the cheap peace of a satisfied curiosity.

He could not think why it was that he had

drifted away from the party to find himself once more in a garden in northern France which he had not seen in more than ten years, nor why it was he should feel in the midst of all these people so utterly detached and so lonely. He was not drunk. He had not been really drunk since the war, when you drank out of boredom or because it eased your nerves or because it gave you a false recklessness. Perhaps it was simply nostalgia, for the sudden vision had left him detached and calm, with that strange feeling of agreeable melancholy touched by a sense of physical illness which is the essence of nostalgia. And it was odd, too, that when the vision of the garden had come to him, it was the vision of an empty garden. Eliane was not there. It was quite empty; the windows were open as if the house were lived in; the fallen leaves of the plane trees were raked into little heaps by some one who must have vanished only a moment before, because the breeze had not yet scattered them again. But it was empty.

He thought, "I feel fed up," and suddenly he was aware that for a long time he had been feeling miserable and restless and unhappy and bored without ever knowing it. The fact that he knew it now, suddenly in the midst of a party, alarmed him.

Jimmy Beaumont was talking. He had been talking all along, and somehow Tom had been able to answer him, even though he had not listened at all and been absorbed by a whole procession of thought which Jimmy wouldn't have understood at all, or would have scoffed at even if he had understood. It was odd how Jimmy respected the results of talent without ever understanding the processes which gave birth to them in the end. Jimmy was a nice, cosy, sensual animal. There wasn't anything romantic about him. Whenever he found it, in whatever form, love was always satisfactory, like a good beefsteak or a fine glass of brandy.

"I like the idea for the new play," he was saying. "Will it be ready for October?"

"I should think so," said Tom. "I've been working on it. It's going very well—better than I had hoped."

Which was all a lie, because he hadn't been working on it at all. It was one of his weaknesses that he always gave the answer that people wanted to hear. Sometimes it was the true one, but more often it was not. Most people liked it that way. It was one of the reasons, he fancied, why most people liked him and why so many came to him with their troubles. It was not, after all, sincerity that they wanted, but to be told what they wanted to hear and to have a chance to talk about themselves. A little shamefully he thought, "I've always been that way—wanting people to like me. Maybe all successful men like that. Maybe in some way they put it over on the rest of the world."

But he suspected that Jimmy did not always believe him.

"Don't let us down," he was saying. "We're all counting on it."

[14]

Tom felt suddenly irritable. "Have I ever let you down?"

"Sometimes you make people believe you haven't let them down when you have." Tommy grinned. "Better look out. Some day you may get found out."

And for the first time Tom pulled himself back into reality and asked, "What makes you say that?"

"Nothing," said Jimmy. "Only you never can tell." Then after a silence, he said, "The woman will be a great part for Maisie."

"I don't agree with you. The way I see it, it isn't Maisie's part at all. It needs an actress who is less intelligent and something of a ham. Maisie hasn't got enough feeling."

"Don't kid yourself about that," said Jimmy. "If Maisie could ever let go, there wouldn't be another actress in the world half as good. She's too cerebrial."

Tom wanted to laugh, but he controlled himself through habit. Long ago he had grown used

to Jimmy's liking for big words and his inca-
pacity to pronounce them properly. There was
something about big words which hypnotized
Jimmy and filled him with awe. Something, too,
made him incapable of using them casually.
Perhaps it was because Jimmy had drawn all his
education from life rather than from a school-
room.

"Well, Maisie thinks it's just the ticket for
her."

"Well, it isn't. She's got no emotional
quality."

"You're wrong there."

"Well, I ought to know."

And then he was aware that for the first time
he had admitted to Jimmy what Jimmy had
known for months—that he and Maisie were
lovers. He caught the hint of a twinkle in
Jimmy's eye and ignored it. Six weeks ago he
would have responded, but now he could not.
Nor could he say to Jimmy, "I don't want
Maisie, because it's all washed up between us

and we're separating on Tuesday for good."
Even Maisie didn't know that—yet.

After a time Jimmy said, "You say that girl
hasn't any emotional quality? Look at her."

At the far end of the room Maisie had begun
to dance. The Viennese music had stopped and
the burden been taken up by the two best hot
piano-players in the world, and they were doing
their best for Maisie, and Maisie was dancing
as only Maisie could when she had had too much
champagne. She was an actress and not a dancer,
but on those rare occasions when she danced
there was something flame-like and exciting in
the spectacle which few professional dancers
ever achieved. There was an awkward grace and
fire about her dancing, as if she found no release
whatever through being an excellent actress, but
only when she had drunk so much that she no
longer cared what she did. At such times the
intellectual comédienne became a bacchante
with a flawless technique.

She was dressed in a plain gown of black

with a narrow bit of poison-green ribbon for a girdle, and she wore no jewels. It was as if she dared to say to all the other women in the room, "I don't need those things," and indeed, thought Tom, she did not. Her red hair and her camellia-white skin were enough. Now as she danced wildly, shaking her hips and waving her arms, the shining red hair tossed about her head. Watching her, he thought, "She is the last of the actresses in the grand tradition. The others all try so damned hard to be ladies instead of actresses that in the end they only give the effect of refined old maids." There was a fire inside her. He knew that Jimmy was right, no matter how many times he denied it, and, after all, who should know better than himself.

Her dancing disturbed him not only because he disliked her making a spectacle of herself and so becoming vulnerable to the all-too-clever tongues of the other women and of Sally in particular, but because there was something ominous in it and because, in spite of anything

he could tell himself to the contrary, it made
her infinitely attractive. Only once before during the months they had been together had she
danced thus in public, and then on an occasion
when they had quarreled. When she went out
with him she never drank too much, because
he did not like her to. Now for a second time
something had gone wrong, some element, some
force which he had overlooked since that first
night he had gone home with her to become
her lover.

As he watched her, trying to divine what it
was that had set her off, the suspicion slowly
dawned on him that she was unhappy and that
she was unhappy because she was in love with
him. Once or twice before he had suspected it
for a moment, but he had always put the idea
away from him because he did not want to accept it. By being in love he meant something
profound which made him uncomfortable. He
did not mean a relationship like all those he
had known since the war and like what he had

believed it would be with Maisie when it began,
but something less amusing and cynical, something which was—he searched for the word and
then accepted it—frightening. He meant the
thing which makes one person the slave of another, a thing compounded at once of delight
and misery, of torture and of a satisfaction so
profound that nothing else in the world com-
pared with it. For a long time he had avoided
falling in love, turning away from it while there
was still time, because it made life so complicated and difficult; and now the intimation of
it returned at the very moment when he had
planned to say a quiet farewell to Maisie and
slip gently away from her, never to see her again
save in the rôle of an old friend. She was making
a spectacle of herself because she was miserable
and she was miserable because she had divined
what it was that he planned to do. It was the
last thing he wanted . . . that thing which not
more than one or two of the clever, brilliant,
successful people in this room had ever known.

They were all afraid of it, and he was himself no different from the others. The music was jazz now and not Viennese waltzes.

And suddenly they seemed, all of them, trivial and even pitiable, himself most of all.

He thought again how odd it was that a man could have won everything for himself in life and still be so helpless and so—again he searched for the word and accepted it— frightened. That was it. He was frightened. There was nothing to be gained by dishonesty. He was frightened, why or of what he did not know, but there it was. Dread hung over him like an illness. The party was going well. It had taken itself out of his hands and he was the only person in the room who was not enjoying it. He found himself grinding his teeth and thinking, "I can't bear it any longer." But what it was he could not bear he was unable to say.

Maisie finished dancing and took out a comb and arranged her hair. The dark piano-player was wiping his hands again and the other one was lighting a cigarette. Maisie leaned across the polished top of the piano, talking to them, and her charm overcame him suddenly and he knew what it was. She was marvelously common, with that immense human commonness of the theater which seemed to him the greatest of qualities. In her it had been miraculously preserved out of the centuries since the first traveling player had set out to entertain. There was nothing bogus, nothing refined, about her. In her naturalness she was complete, a thing which gave satisfaction. Watching her as she leaned across the piano, talking to the dark Jewish boy with the long nose, he noticed really for the first time the beauty and perfection of her body, of her hands, of her feet, a miracle which had come out of an immigrant Irish family living in a squalid street on the West Side. There was a look of race about her, in the way she moved, in the fineness of her bones—Maisie Dantry, born plain Mary Hennessey, who had begun life at seventeen as a chorus girl. And then he looked away from her sharply, fearful that she might regain the hold she had had over him for a little while months ago.

And then from the stairway Sally came into the room with Malcolm James. She looked well —too well, he thought—with that smartness which Frenchwomen attain, in which all charm and softness is sacrificed to artificiality. In all her blond prettiness she was too perfect, so that her personality was lost in an inhuman assortment of sequins and slippers and jewels. Lately the sight of Sally nearly always gave him a faint shock, as if she were a stranger to him, but without the interest which might attach to a stranger. About her he had no curiosity whatever, for in his own mind he had determined long ago that he knew all there was to know. He would find himself wondering why it was that he had ever married her when they had so little in common. He could not quite fix the reason, but he knew that it was not because he was in love with her, so in love that he must have her one way or another. There had never been any of that on her side, either. And here she was with Malcolm James in tow, square, stolid, red-faced, dull Malcolm James, the only person at the party who was not clever. He felt no jealousy of Malcolm. If he felt anything at all, it was contempt for his dullness, yet the sight of him with Sally always irritated him, pricking his vanity that Sally could even look at Malcolm, let alone find him attractive, when her husband was about. But that, he decided, was probably exactly the way she felt about Maisie, so everyone came off even. Once long ago Malcolm must have been attractive in a physical way, with high color and clear eyes—the sort of boy who made all the best clubs and had a kind of animal charm which went with youth and afterward disappeared as he solidified into conventional middle age. New York was full of men like him, who went to the office at nine and returned home by way of the club to dine out at eight. They scarcely thought at all save to watch the market. Their interior existence, Tom thought, scornfully, must be *nil*.

The uprise of his scorn for Malcolm, oddly enough, made him feel less depressed. He tried to discover what was the matter with his life. He had a wife whom he did not love, but on the other hand she made no trouble, because long ago they had come to an arrangement, both going their own ways without so much as discussing it. And he had two sons, and he had all the money he needed, and his capital lay not in banks which might fail nor in stocks which could vanish, but in his own head, and so he could never lose it save by madness or death, and both these things seemed very remote. He had the health of a truck-driver and the energy of a steam-engine. Only one thing had failed him, and that, strangely enough, seemed to be life itself.

While he sat there people came and went, exchanging words with him which he answered mechanically, like an automaton, and all the while Jimmy Beaumont sat there, sometimes silent, watching the crowd, sometimes talking. No one, not even Jimmy, who knew him so well with that infallible animal instinct of his, seemed to notice that he was any different inside. None of them was clever enough to see that *something* had happened to him—something which had been coming on for a long time. The most they said was, "You look tired tonight, Tom," and he wasn't tired. He could go on all night and all the next day and think nothing of it. There wasn't anything wrong with his body. What fools these clever people were!

But, anyway, he could escape very shortly now. He didn't any longer expect much in the way of escape from travel, because no matter where you went you always had yourself to take along. He could pack up and on Tuesday he could say good-by to Maisie, quietly and casually, when she went off to the Coast to make a picture, and she would never know that it was all over and finished forever. The strain of pre-

tending that he was still in love or that he was
even still interested would be over and he would
be free again, moving from London to Paris, to
Vienna, to the south of France. He would write
to her and let her down slowly, because he hated
scenes and partings and anything which touched
his emotions very profoundly.

He had been clever about that, all his life,
since he was twenty-one, never to allow himself to get into a jam through his emotions.
Nothing had ever gotten in his way, nothing
had ever ruined him as it had plenty of other
fellows. And now Maisie had turned female and
primitive and unpredictable. She might even
change something which had begun as a lark
into something that was troublesome and tragic.

He saw her coming toward him, and again
he was aware of her perfection. She trained like
an athlete and went through all sorts of beauty
nonsense because it was part of her career to
keep her figure and to look as young as possible,
and so as a rule she looked handsome and per-

fectly ageless. Tonight she seemed flushed and young. As she came toward him all the wild gaiety that had been in her dancing seemed to go out of her. She came and sat down beside him, almost with apology, like a small girl who has been naughty and wishes to atone. He liked her best when she was like this, and she was nearly always like this when they were alone. The dazzling, hard, brilliant Maisie known to the public and the world and parties like this seemed to melt and disappear when she was with him.

"Take me home," she said, abruptly. "I'm dying on my feet."

He did not want to take her home, because once he was in her flat they might begin to talk, and slowly but surely she might discover his plans. For the first time since he had known her her presence made him restless and uneasy. It was as if something had slipped from his control.

"I can't go now. After all, it's my party, and yours, too, in a way."

"The party's all right. It'll take care of itself. Nobody will miss you. You certainly haven't been a ball of fire tonight. What's the matter with you?"

"Nothing." There was no use trying to explain what he himself did not understand.

"Take me home," she said again, urgently. "Nobody will miss him, will they, Jimmy?"

"No," said Jimmy, with a great deal of detachment, as if he had no intention of becoming involved in the matter.

Then Tom was silent for a moment, thinking. Perhaps if he took her home now he wouldn't have to go again on Tuesday night, before she went away. Maybe they could settle things quietly. Maybe the whole thing would solve itself. Maybe all his dread of a scene, all his terror of weakening simply to keep her from scorning him was merely nerves.

"All right," he said, dully, "you go downstairs. I'll meet you in your motor."

When she had gone he remained for a moment, taking one more look at the party. It was true, what she said. It would take care of itself. Everybody had champagne and caviar, sausages and bacon, chicken in aspic. They didn't need him at all. They wouldn't even notice that he had gone. Perhaps if he never came back, they wouldn't notice, either. Everything was all right so long as he was rich and successful. But if once he slipped, even for a moment, they would forget him as if he had never existed.

Then he had a glimpse of Sally and Malcolm James starting up the stairway at the end of the room, going up to some other room where they might be alone. Dully he was aware that he did not care what she and Malcolm did, and almost at once the knowledge made him feel a little ill. For four or five years the two of them had led their own lives, going out together whenever it was necessary, giving parties together, and sometimes not seeing each other for days, even though they lived in the same house. It had come about simply because there had never been time to think of what was happening. He had never considered until this moment that it might be messy and awful and without dignity.

Quietly he put down his glass and went down the stairs, out of the door into the street, where Maisie's car was waiting in the warm summer night. When he climbed in beside her she didn't say anything, but only took his hand and pressed it gently. When they were halfway to her flat she said, softly: "Anything gone wrong? Anything I can do to help?"

Without moving his body, his spirit drew away from her. For sixteen years he had gone his own way, dependent upon no one for money or strength or sympathy or even tenderness. When people offered him any of these things he had been grateful, but very quietly he had turned away from them, and now he could do nothing else.

After that Maisie was silent, and as the motor drew up to the curb, she said, "I'm sorry I made an ass of myself tonight." And immediately his instinct was to disclaim even his right of criticism lest it make their relationship seem something more profound than he meant it to be.

"You have every right to make an ass of yourself. I don't like it, but you are quite experienced enough to know what you want to do."

After midnight there was no elevator boy in the house, and so they piloted themselves up alone, in silence. It was only when they were inside the flat and she had closed the door behind them that she spoke. Then she threw off her coat and said, "I'm so glad to be away from all those awful people." And throwing her arms about him, she pressed herself close to him, kissing him with a curious nervous passion which upset him.

"What's the matter?" he asked.

"I can't bear to leave you."

He began almost at once to lie. "It won't be for long, only for the summer. I'd go with you, but I'd go crazy in Hollywood. I hate it."

He remained standing near the door without

putting down his hat, as if to tell her that he meant to go quickly home, but she said: "Stay here tonight. Please, darling, stay. I've got the jitters. I'm afraid to stay alone."

Again the thought occurred to him that if he stayed tonight he might not have to return on Tuesday and go through it all. It did not matter whether he stayed or not, for, whatever happened, he knew that he would find neither surprise nor disappointment.

"All right. Let's have a drink."

It was after four o'clock when he rose from the bed and turned on the lamp. Almost at once she sat up and asked, "Where are you going?"

He sat on the edge of the bed, lighted a cigarette, and said, quietly, "Home."

For a moment she looked at him in silence, and then in a voice sharp with bitterness she said: "Yes, you can always do that. You're very clever. You keep a place called home that you can escape to whenever things become boring or

[33]

difficult. I see why you stick to Sally. I should have thought this was your home."

And then he knew that he would not escape without a scene, and suddenly he felt hopelessly exhausted, as if all the spirit had been drained out of him.

"It wasn't like that ever, Maisie. You've got to be honest. We never pretended it was. I'm married and I've got the two boys."

"Yes. I can see what use Sally is to you. I see why you stick to her. She's very useful when you want to get away."

Quietly he put his hand over hers on the coverlet. "Don't be like that, Maisie. You're too good to behave like that. I'm not going home to Sally —you ought to know that—and I'm not trying to get out of anything. I'm going home to shut myself in and lock the door and be alone."

Her silence told him that he had hurt her and that made him know that she looked upon whatever it was that existed between them as something far deeper than he had ever held it to be.

She was offering him everything she had to offer
—love, sympathy, tenderness. She had given him
her body long ago, but he had known for years
that bodies were unimportant and meant nothing. It was what went with them that mattered.

"I didn't mean to hurt you. Sometimes I'm
like that. Sometimes things become intolerable
and then there's nothing for it but for me to be
by myself."

"What's intolerable?" she asked.

"I don't know. I can't tell you because I don't
know, myself, but at the moment it's the one
thing I want most in the world."

"It's hard when you push me away like that.
All I want to do is help you and make life easy
for you. I love you more than anything, my dear,
more even than I love myself and that is saying
something."

Instead of answering her he pressed her hand
quietly. Then, afraid that he would hurt her
more deeply, he crushed out his cigarette and
went into the other room to dress; but when he

came back she was still sitting up in bed and she was crying without making a sound.

"Don't do that, Maisie," he said. "It doesn't mean anything. I'm going away because I have to. We'll go on seeing each other."

But she wasn't to be fooled and deep in his heart he knew that it was ridiculous of him ever to have believed that he could let her down easily and escape before she understood what was happening. She wasn't like most of the women he had known, simply vain and foolish and very often trivial. She wasn't bred in luxury, a useless, silly creature. She had made her own life, just as he had made his, and out of it had come knowledge and wisdom. Nor was she innocent and without experience. She had known men before she had ever seen him. Standing at the end of the bed, looking down at her, he felt sorry for her and disgusted with himself and the whole miserable scene, but at the same time he thought: "I mustn't pity her, because then I'll be betrayed. I won't know what

I'm doing and afterward I'll find myself caught and tied down." And in the midst of his thoughts he understood suddenly how it was he had been caught by Sally. He had been sorry for her, and by the time he learned that pity was the last thing Sally had need of, there were two children and it was too late.

"Tom," she said, "listen to me."

"I'm listening."

"Sit down there on the end of the bed. I won't do anything stupid, I promise." She dried her eyes. "I've had too tough a life to use tricks on anybody, least of all on you. Anyway, you know when I'm acting and when I'm not."

"Yes." He lighted another cigarette and sat down, distantly, prepared to listen, thinking that nothing on earth could alter his determination and that somehow it was wrong and shameful to let her throw herself against the wall of his indifference and caution. It would be humiliating for both of them, but he was too weary to stop her.

"There isn't anybody else, is there?"

"No, there isn't anybody else." And as he spoke he knew that at the moment there was no woman he knew nor any he could ever imagine who would have the power to stir him.

"Are you fed up?"

"No, my dear. I think you're the most attractive woman I know."

"Darling, I love you. I'm going to tell you what I never told any other man. I've never been in love before. I never had any idea what it was like."

He could not tell her that this was a foolish statement, because, having tried before, she had every reason to know. She had lived like a man, yet, being a woman, she still had a capacity for falling profoundly in love. Only a woman could do that. He did not know what to say and so he said nothing.

"I mean that," she said. "I'd do anything in the world for you, anything you want." Suddenly she wasn't crying any more and she had a

kind of dignity he had not seen in her before,
and there was a curious light in her face which
made him uneasy because, after all, he was re-
sponsible for it, and it was a responsibility from
which it was very difficult to escape. The faintly
mocking, cynical, entertaining Maisie seemed to
have vanished.

"Do you know what it is to be in love? To sit
up waiting until some one turns the key in the
lock? To think of no one else? To be happy
when he's in the same room with you and miserable when he's not? Do you know what it is
to go about saying to yourself: 'I won't let him
keep such a hold on me. I must escape from
him,' and then never be able to escape? I wasn't
drunk tonight. I knew what I was doing. I
made a fool of myself because I was so unhappy
that I thought maybe that was a way of saving
myself, for a little while, anyway. Whenever
I've been nasty to you it was because I loved
you so much that I couldn't bear it. Can't you
imagine how terrible that is for a woman who

has never been caught by anyone, who's always been selfish and egotistical? I'd do anything for you—anything you want."

He did not answer her at once, and when he did speak it was with an honesty brutal not only to her but to himself. "The trouble is, my dear, that there isn't anything you can do. You see, there isn't anything I want."

She looked at him in silence, and after a moment she said, in a low voice: "But that's awful! That's horrible! It's like being already dead!"

She had described it—exactly what the thing was which terrified him. "Yes," he said, "it's pretty awful. You see that's what is the matter with me."

"Will you let me try to help you?"

"No. I can't bear that from anyone."

"Is it as bad as that?" He didn't answer her and she went on: "Do you hate me? Are you bored with me?"

"No, it isn't like that at all. I don't feel anything except fondness and respect and admiration. I'm very fond of you, Maisie."

Then the bitterness returned to her voice. "But you've got everything out of me you can get and now you've got to find somebody or something else."

"No, it's worse than that. I don't want anybody. I don't think any woman would interest me and I've got to be alone and have peace. Everything has got to going faster and faster. I have to stop. I have to." And suddenly, inexplicably the vision of the old house and the garden leading down to the river came to him again. Peace. That was it. Peace.

She was thoughtful for a time and then she said: "I didn't think it was going to end like this. I didn't think I'd ever be caught or I never would have begun. I didn't want to fall in love with you. You're so sweet and gentle and charming. Why are you like that?"

He thought for a moment, and again he had a moment of cold honesty. He heard himself saying a truth which had occurred to him a little earlier in the evening for the first time in his life. "I suppose it's because I want people to like me. That's part of it. I've always been like that—all things to all people. I suppose it's a weakness and a strength all at the same time."

"It wasn't because you loved me, then?"

"No. That part was real. But I'd have been just the same if I hadn't loved you."

"When did it change?"

"I don't know. It changed gradually."

"After you got what you wanted?"

"Yes, I suppose so. I've always been bored as soon as I got what I wanted." And he felt ashamed of himself suddenly, for the first time since he was a boy.

"You won't act, will you?" she asked. "You aren't saying these things just to make yourself interesting?"

"No, not now. I might have once. I did once —quite often because it amused me—not these same things, because they never occurred to me until this moment, but other things like them. I used to write mental dialogues like that—saying something—acting a part to see what people would say and how they would respond. I used to do it up till the moment I came in the door tonight. But I very rarely did it with you, my dear, because you're much too smart."

"Haven't you ever thought about yourself?"

"No. Quite honestly no. I've always been too busy and too interested in people and things."

"I think it's just as well."

"Why?"

"Because if you ever thought about yourself for long, it would be horrible." The tears had vanished, and in their place bitterness had returned. "Because you're a monster, Tom. But I love you very much. I'm a bit of a monster myself. All successful people are. It's because I'm so much in love with you that I'd give up everything for you that I'm afraid. I'm afraid for yourself. If I didn't love you I wouldn't much care what became of you." He hadn't looked at

[43]

her for a long time now, and he heard what she was saying only through the fog of his own confused thoughts. Presently he heard her voice again.

"Haven't you ever been in love? I mean the way I am now—so that nothing else in the world matters at all?"

"Yes," he said.

"Sally?"

"No."

"I see."

"It was somebody you'll never see. Somebody you've never even heard of. So there's no one to be jealous of. I don't even know where she is."

"But that doesn't make any difference, except envy. I only envy her because you would be so lovely if you could really love some one." She spoke sadly, leaning a little toward him as if she could not help herself. "God has given you so much—looks and charm and success and vitality —and you give so little back. You keep it all to use for yourself. Kiss me good night and then

[44]

go home and lock yourself in and be alone. Some day you'll find out that nobody—not even you or me—can live like that. You see I've only just found it out."

He only said, "No, I won't kiss you," without moving, and when she asked him why, he said, "Because it's better not, for both of us." He got up from the bed. "But I think I'd better go home now."

"You haven't heard anything I said."

"Yes, I have." But it was hardly true.

"Will I see you again?"

"I think it's better not—not before you go away."

"Good night."

"Good night."

Closing the door after him, he went out into the hall, aware of a curious feeling of dullness, as if all his senses were numbed. Neither the sight of Maisie, weeping and then angry, nor the bitter things which she said, made any impression whatever. He seemed to see her and hear her bitterness from a great distance, without its touching him. "Yes," he thought, "it is true, what she says. So what?" But it had gone off well, almost easily, with less violence and hysteria than he had expected, leaving him sorry for her. But there was nothing he could do without being caught, and he had to be free now, and alone.

He closed the door of the flat quietly behind him and pressed the button of the automatic elevator, but before it arrived he heard the door opening behind him and, turning, he saw Maisie standing there in her nightdress. There was a look of physical anguish in her eyes, so clear and unmistakable that he was astonished, thinking, "I didn't know it was so bad as that."

"Don't go, Tom," she said. "Don't go. If you go, I'll chuck everything. I'll die. Inside me, I'll die. Don't look at me like that. I'm not dirt under your feet. Don't go. You can't hurt me like this. Don't go, Tom."

He tried to talk to her, but a terrible numbness took possession of him again and all he could say was, "Don't, Maisie. Don't——"

The elevator was there and all that remained for him to do in order to escape was to step inside and close the door. Pressing the button, he began to slip downward, but in the second before he disappeared out of sight he saw her face again. In her eyes there was a look of astonishment in which there was something childish and naïve, as if instead of being a tired experienced woman of thirty-eight she were a little girl of seventeen. Then he was gone, and he thought: "I can't be kind any longer. I'm too tired. Anyway, it wouldn't do any good."

Outside, the air was cooler now and there were millions of stars shining, only a little dimmed by the first light of dawn. As far as he could see, both in the direction of the river and in that of the Park, the street was empty and silent. From a long way off there came the faint hoarse sound of a ship's whistle. Turning, he set out toward the Park, walking quickly, a little astonished that New York could ever be so still that you could hear the echo of your own footsteps, back and forth from building to building. There was something irritating in the sound, and as he walked it seemed to grow louder and louder so that each step jarred his nerves, interrupting his thoughts.

This was the city he loved above all else in the world, *his* New York, to which he had come long ago, alone, knowing no one, to find his way. And as he walked the memory of the city as he had first seen it returned to him, its towers rising out of the gray mist of a winter morning. And he tried to imagine what it had been like, sixteen years ago, to walk along the street alone as he was doing now, without having a friend in the whole city, with the whole of the adventure still before him, but the sensation was difficult to recapture, and all he saw was a big rawboned boy, fresh out of the army, excitable, restless, ambitious, still bewildered by what had

[48]

happened to him in the gray house by the edge
of the river, hurt and lonely and yet exhilarated
and triumphant in the knowledge of his own
freedom and strength. He could remember what
the boarding-house on lower Lexington Avenue
was like and even vaguely the shabby furnish-
ings of the room where sometimes on the hot
summer nights he had sat in the window, watching the people in the streets, happy as he had
always been simply in the awareness of life
going on about him. It was odd how that feeling had gone lately, odd how indifferent he had
become to people, as if a shell had been growing about him slowly, imperceptibly.

But he could not, try as he would, remember
what it felt like long ago, nor even very clearly
those first friends he had made, here and there
by hazard, the way one makes friends in a great
blowsy city like New York. For a moment he
would see a face, disembodied and rather ghost-
like, without name or background, or perhaps
remember a name which was only a word, float-

ing in space, attached to nothing. Nearly all of
them had slipped away, vanished in confusion.
Some of them—a very few—he had seen since,
one or two newspapermen who, like himself,
had succeeded, but most of the faces which returned to him were those of men who had come
to him timidly in failure or with a brazenness
which covered the limp despair of defeat, to ask
for help; and he had always given it to them,
because he had so much and it was so easy, and
it made them like you for a little time at least,
and it left you with such a pleasant feeling afterward. Nearly always they said that they had
been unlucky, but that he knew was less than
the truth. In that sudden clarity of vision which
came over him as he sat on the edge of Maisie's
bed he saw that he had been no luckier than the
rest of them, save in the strength and health of
his body. He was no more intelligent than most
of them, and a good deal less clever than many;
but he had worked, learning how to be clever
and to protect himself and get what he wanted,

because he had had such a hunger for success. He had learned how to be successful and he had always known what he wanted, and the others had scarcely ever known. After that it was easy, so damned easy that it was boring.

But it was very difficult to remember what it was like to be poor and lonely and hopeful. It was all too far away and there were too many faces in between, faces of every race and nationality, from America and all of Europe and even the Orient. They were all very different, but they had one thing in common—they were the faces of successful people, and so they were different from the faces he had known when young. It was odd how as you won success you were removed little by little, imperceptibly, away from the rest of the world, until at last you lost the feel and even the savor of ordinary pleasant things and became a little inhuman, so that, even though you made a great effort to establish once more a contact with the simple ones—the plodders, the dull ones, the failures—it was not pos-

[51]

sible. It was as if they would no longer accept you. Somehow you found yourself shut into a dubious fantastic paradise surrounded only by those who had succeeded.

Turning into Park Avenue, he encountered two scrubwomen on their way to work, gray, shapeless bundles they were, wearing odd bedraggled hats which had come all the way from Paris through parties and dust-bins to strike the fancy of these two old ladies. As they passed him one of them was telling a story: "And I said, 'Well, for Gawd's sake, what did you expect?' " and the other one laughed. He looked after them and then was aware that he was being followed along the curb by a taxicab.

"No, thanks," he said to the driver, and in response from under a checked cap a Negro face answered: "Okay boss! It's a fine morning for a constitutional."

He was lonely suddenly and full of envy at the easy friendliness of the two old hags and the taxi-driver. That was what he wanted to recover

—that and a great deal more. The odd thing was that while he envied them something which had gone out of his life, neither the scrubwomen nor the Negro taxi-driver would envy him at all, except for his money. And then he knew why he, who never walked anywhere, had chosen to walk all the way from Maisie's flat to his own home. It was because this was the first time in a year that he had stopped moving, so fast that there had never been any time for thought or reflection. Somehow, since the moment he had had the odd vision of the still, gray old house time had stood still. He was aware of himself, for the first time, as a person apart from all the confusion. The boy crossing on the ferryboat toward the last dying light of Manhattan was sixteen years away and yet appallingly near. What, he thought, has happened to me since then? All that time he had been frantically active, yet nothing had happened at all. Really, nothing had happened since he was twenty-one, and on his next birthday he would be thirty-eight.

[53]

Maisie was right. In that there was something monstrous.

As he came in sight of his own house he saw three figures come out of the doorway and step into a taxicab, and at sight of them he slipped into an areaway to watch without being seen, hoping that they were the last and that the party was over. He knew it was impossible to go back to the party. Perhaps he could never again return to the party. He thought, "I have had enough and too much." He could not bear the thought of their wise-cracks and their clever, brittle, malicious talk, the expensive clothes and jewels of the women, all that curious hardness that enveloped them and set them apart, making them a little less than human.

He walked as far as the Park and back, waiting for the lights to be put out inside the house, and when he returned it was in darkness.

Letting himself in, he switched on the lights and climbed the stairs to the big room. For a moment he hesitated, wondering whether he could find his way through the wreckage of the party, in darkness, to his own stairway, so that he would not have to see the disordered room; and then, counting this as weakness, he turned on the lights.

The tired servants had left everything untouched for the morning, and the wreckage was still there. Around the fireplace there were little heaps of cigarette butts. Some one had broken a glass and pushed the shattered fragments under the edge of the sofa. In another corner a cushion stained with champagne had been placed against the radiator to dry. There were glasses everywhere and even a plate or two with the remnants of *pâté de foie gras* and caviar, and on the floor beneath the piano lay a handkerchief of green chiffon. He knew it at once—the handkerchief Maisie had been using in her wild dance. For a moment he stood looking down at it, and then quietly he pushed the piano aside, picked up the handkerchief, and thrust it into his pocket. Then he turned out the lights and went up the small winding stairway to his own room.

But when he had undressed he could not sleep, and after a time he rose and climbed the stairs at the back of the house where the two boys occupied a room so far removed that the noise of their parents' parties belowstairs could not disturb them. It was Nanny who had arranged that, sternly, as she arranged everything which had to do with his two sons—their health, their education, their amusements, their very souls. As he climbed the stairs he thought of her humorously, as he always did even when there were disputes and words, and affectionately because she was an irresistible character and stood for something which he respected profoundly. She represented everything which was stable in a world which moved so fast that sometimes it made you giddy. Wherever she went, a little island of peace, order, and efficiency surrounded her. Waves of confusion beat against it but never overwhelmed it. She managed to create order and peace in the most unlikely places—in the midst of the utmost confusion, on piers and aboard ocean liners, in fashionable hotels and on beaches littered with naked bodies. She had no awe of customs officials or porters or *concierges* or policemen. She was always in the right and that was sufficient. She was the rock of ages who brought peace and order to his house, to his children, and often enough even to himself. No matter where they were nor what went on, Nanny and the two boys and their Scotties Hustler and Dash went their orderly way, a solemn, half-comic and terribly important procession. It occurred to him suddenly how odd it was that a middle-aged woman of great character named Jessie Simpson, born in the Orkney Islands, should be caring for two boys who were the children of Sally, who was born in Eighth Street, New York, and had spent all her life in fashionable hotels, and himself, an orphan farmer boy from Illinois and

[57]

an *arriviste* of the first order. It was lucky he had her to guard his boys against that strange, giddy, false world which surrounded them, to guard them, he thought, ruefully, even against their own brilliant, successful, busy father.

At the foot of the last flight of stairs he kicked off his slippers and walked barefoot, lest the sound of his footsteps rouse her or the boys and bring her stalwart figure in wrapper and curl papers to open the door and attack him. He was afraid of Nanny, not because there was anything about her which really terrified him, but because she was always so profoundly right and so, without speaking, made him feel a fool and ashamed of himself. If she wakened, she would scold him for coming to the nursery at such an hour and she would be right, and although she could not possibly know that he came there straight from the bed of Maisie, she would somehow give him the impression that she knew what he had been up to and put him utterly to rout by a single glance of her clear blue eyes.

He was not altogether sure that she would not divine the truth, knowing it by instinct in the canny, disconcerting fashion of the Scot.

Scarcely breathing, he managed to pass her door in safety and quietly opened the door of the night nursery. The shades were partly drawn, but there was enough light for him to distinguish the figures of the two boys beneath the blankets of their beds on opposite sides of the small room. Peter, who was rather like his mother, had blond hair, and young Tom, who was like himself, was dark, with a stubborn chin and lips. As he closed the door young Tom stirred and threw one small arm across his eyes.

It was a simple gesture, without significance, but something about it touched him profoundly, and for a moment he experienced one of those rare moments when an indescribable love for them took possession of him. Perhaps it was rooted in the idea of their helplessness and the knowledge that they were dependent upon him and under his protection until they were old enough to begin life in their own ways. Partly, too, he knew that he loved them because he had begot them and they belonged to himself; they were small extensions of his own ego, even of his own body. There were long periods when he scarcely thought of them at all, and times even when their presence could annoy him, and then there were those moments of curious, almost voluptuous, affection for them. Looking down at them, it occurred to him that perhaps he loved them less for themselves than because they were small patterns of himself, and so a part of all those ambitious plans which had begun so long ago when he was not much older than they were now. He thought, "I must have been thirteen or fourteen when I first knew that I had to subdue the world."

Standing there beside them in the expensive nursery, the memory of his own childhood returned to him, so distant and so different from the life of his own sons. He had never had a Nanny, but only Aunt Cassie, who was always so busy with her garden and the canning and the chickens that there was little time left for him, only enough to keep him clean and, as far as possible, neatly dressed. And he had never had two rooms to himself, with bookcases filled with books and cupboards stuffed with toys. And there wasn't any fashionable new-fangled school, but only a small weatherbeaten school-house with an iron stove to which he walked three miles and back alone in every kind of weather. And there was no talk of diets and of certified milk. He had always eaten what the others ate, Aunt Cassie and the farmhands and the hired girl, and all the same he had grown up tough and lean and strong, with that un-quenchable vitality and indestructible health which came down to him on both sides of the family.

He did not envy them at all, for he had known delights which they would never know —the look of the fields and the distant wood on a frosty October morning, and threshing-day

with the table under the catalpa trees and Aunt
Cassie swishing away the flies while the neigh-
boring farmers, shining with soap and water,
ate and their wives carried out mountains of
food to serve them. And he remembered feeding the small calves out of a pail when they were
bigger than you were and sometimes knocked
you down and spilled all the warm milk, and
the delight of fishing along the creek and swimming for the first time in April when the water
was still icy cold. But above all they never knew
a whole landscape with intimacy. Already they
knew half the scenery of Europe and a great
deal of America, but they had never known, and
probably never would know, one piece of land
in which every hedge and ditch, every bend in
the stream, every tree and stick and stone, belonged to you alone, making a secret world
which you shared with no one.

None of these things would they ever know,
and all the expensive things which they had in
the place of them seemed to him pallid and

anemic in comparison. They could never have
what he had had, because their father had been
a great success, and now there was no way of
turning back from that. Wherever they went,
whatever they did, their world would always be
different from his own, and so they would never
see things as he saw them. They would grow
up in a world where half of what he had had to
learn would be accepted by them as humdrum
and everyday and uninteresting, and so they
would miss a great deal of the richness of life.
The excitement of discovery and the wonder of
finding out for oneself would be denied them.

"I've had luck," he thought. "I'm the perfect
success story. I've seen the works. I've had all
the fun." And then suddenly he was startled by
the knowledge that without thinking of it he
had placed all that in the past, as if it were over
forever. And again the short cynical phrase
occurred to him: "I've had everything. So
what?"

Only Americans could have invented that

brief, terrifying, and inclusive phrase, "So what?" It was born out of their own life and civilization, out of their hunger for experience and excitement, their taste for gambling, their recklessness, their quick and sudden satiation born of exaggerated greediness. All Americans worth their salt were success stories. They had had to overcome obstacles in order to gain the title. Tradition simply did not count, for the only tradition was that there must be no tradition. Those who did not fight did not count for much. Yet in the end there was that terrifying expression, born of their very character and experience, "So what?"

He felt a sudden desire to kiss both boys, lightly on the tops of their small heads, but he dared not do it lest he wake them. If they wakened to find him there, looking down at them sentimentally at this hour of the morning, they would wonder why he had come and he would never be able to tell them. They might even be a little frightened with the fear children have for unbalanced acts born of emotion. He thought, suddenly, "I don't know them at all." In the whole household there was only Nanny who knew them, a stranger from another world; for Sally, he was aware quite without bitterness, knew them even less than himself. For her they were an ornament, a symbol, and she found pleasure not at all in motherhood, but in the picture of herself as a mother, which was quite different. They were handsome ornaments which she might produce now and then dressed up and resentful, as a part of her own smartness and good looks. "Cornelia," he thought sourly, "mother of the Gracchi. These are my jewels!" Perhaps it was too late ever to know them, ever to claim them for his own. He had always been so busy, so occupied with money and fame and vanity, so occupied with clever, distinguished people, that there had never been any time.

He went away at last, picking up his slippers at the bottom of the stairs, and as he passed

Sally's door he stopped for a moment outside, listening and thinking: "What if I opened it and went in. What if I wakened her and said: 'Let's begin again. Let's try to achieve reality. Let's try to build up what has fallen down, if it ever existed. Let's try to live quietly and well in a solid world.'"

But he dared not do it, because in his heart he knew it was too late now. Very likely she would waken and look at him in astonishment and even resentment, and ask him if he had lost his mind. He could not do it, because he knew her too well—that she was incapable of love and even of sensuality. She was only vanity and prettiness. It was possible to become her lover again only through perversity, in cold blood simply to overcome the challenge of her shallowness, to force her to desire him, in a way to corrupt her, sensually with deliberation in order to provide the amusement to make it worth his while. In that at least there was an obstacle and a challenge, but he knew almost at once that he did not care enough to overcome her indifference and mockery. He was too tired.

Somehow, all the women he had known turned out the same in the end. Not Maisie, perhaps, but he was tired of Maisie. *"Plus ça change,"* he thought, and in his fancy he saw Sally asleep in her great gilded bed between the pink embroidered linen sheets she took with her even when traveling, more attractive now and more seductive than when he had married her. She was less confused now, less timid and frightened, but she was also harder and more difficult to reach; and apparently she preferred Malcolm James to himself.

Without entering, he turned away from her door and went to his own room, thinking: "Perhaps I was wrong. Perhaps I should have gone in. Perhaps that would have changed everything." It was odd how shy the thought of entering her room made him feel, shyer even than if she had been a strange woman, for it was a shyness born at once of indifference and fa-

[67]

miliarity. Some people called the way they lived civilized and modern, but now, considering it almost for the first time, he suspected that it was a state of affairs which was simply messy and the result of indolence and indifference and lack of character. He knew now that he had never loved her, not as much as he had loved Maisie in the beginning, or even as much as two or three other women he could think of. She had been convenient and pretty and worldly and had suited his scheme of things, but above all else he had married her because he had felt sorry for her.

He kept thinking of that after he was in bed again in his own room and sleep would not come to him, and he saw her again as he had seen her at Cannes in tow of a mother who was a fool and would not give up and settle into middle age. He saw her again, not the assured, dominating Sally who lay asleep upstairs, secure in her own experience and in the sureness which came of having money and being the wife of a

successful man, but a frightened, silly, sentimental young girl who had never lived anywhere
but in fashionable hotels and villas surrounded
by the sort of people who lived in such places
or the hangers-on of people who could afford it
—silly middle-aged women and elderly men,
near gigolos and stranded Russians and little
Frenchmen with complicated names and titles
whose families expected them to marry American or Jewish heiresses in order to carry on the
prestige of names long since phosphorescent
with decay. It struck him now that the pity he
felt for her in the midst of that *galère* had exactly the same quality as the pity which led some
men to marry prostitutes in the belief that they
could save and reform them. And she, he supposed, found him attractive because he was unlike any man she had ever met. And so that
night in the bar, after she had found a man in
her mother's bedroom and had come downstairs
hysterical, he had asked her to marry him, thinking that he was really in love with her and that

[69]

he could save her by bringing stability into her life.

He knew now that he had not brought stability into her life, but only another kind of confusion, better in quality but very little different in essence. The people he had brought to her were less second rate, but they had the same restlessness. What she had wanted, without knowing it, was security, and there somehow he had failed her. Because he was an adventurer and had always known what he wanted, security meant nothing to him. Security was himself, his own wits and talents and intelligence. But she had none of these things. She appreciated the benefits of success and was greedy for them, without ever understanding the satisfaction of it, as he had always done. He had never taught her anything, and after the first few months he had scarcely even talked to her save when they were dressing in the evening or were on a train when there was nothing else to do, and almost at once she had irritated him by her frivolity, her vanity, and that faint intangible jealousy, not of him, but of his success. And there never had been time for intimacy.

Presently he fell asleep, and when he wakened he did not know how long he had slept, because it had been a period of confusion of which he remembered very little. He was aware that he must have been ill, for in moments of consciousness he saw nurses, at least two of them, because their faces were not the same, and a doctor, and once three doctors, sitting about his bed. And sometimes he was back again on the farm with Aunt Cassie, and again he was in the war. But most of the time he seemed to be in the gray house and the garden which ran down to the river, and then, instead of a strange nurse, Eliane seemed to be beside his bed, looking exactly as she had looked sixteen years before, rather grave and dark, with lips that curled up humorously at the corners, and in her eyes a faint light of mockery at his innocence and

[71]

naïveté. And then suddenly she would be gone, fading out as figures do in cinemas.

It was Sally who told him that he had been ill for nearly a month, so ill that he had come very near to dying. None of the doctors seemed able to make up his mind what it was. Years earlier they might have called it brain fever, but now they talked of "breakdowns" and "collapses" from overwork. Only he himself knew what was wrong with him, and it was no use trying to tell the others, least of all the doctors, for they would not have understood. It occurred to him that if during the illness he had been conscious most of the time, he might have died simply out of boredom, because he had no special desire to live. It made no sense to tell doctors and scientists that it was not your body but your soul which was ill. They would simply say that being fed up couldn't make you so ill as all that; but he knew that he was right, and as he grew stronger he came to understand that he hadn't yet recovered and that he might never recover.

Sally, sitting beside the bed, talking or reading to him out of the newspapers, was brisk and cheerful and full of superficial sympathy. She, he knew, would be the last to understand what was the matter with him, for she was one of those fortunate ones whose lives are so occupied with trivial affairs that there is time left for nothing else. She had her clothes, her engagements for lunch and dinner, her theaters, her meetings with Malcolm James, her appointments with hair-dressers and beauty specialists. Watching her, it struck him how fresh and crisp and contented she seemed, and coldly and with detachment he began to speculate on how much had happened between her and Malcolm. And even though she sat by him, dutifully and cheerfully, he was aware that after a little time she was restless and eager to be off. It was as if she sat there counting the minutes. "It is not very flattering," he thought, "and a long way from those romantic stories about a dangerous illness bringing a husband and wife together again."

And it struck him that if he had died she might have shed a few sentimental tears for the far-distant past and worked herself up romantically, as she had a gift for doing, and then quickly she would have settled back into her own busy life, very smartly dressed in widow's weeds from Schiaparelli. Again it pricked his vanity that he should have success with so many other attractive women and fail to interest his own wife at all.

And the boys came in from time to time to stand shyly by the bed, more distant than they had ever been before because illness seemed strange and unnatural to them and the intimation of death grotesque and frightening. They were bored as children are by people whose vitality has slipped away in illness, and he had not the strength to make a great effort and bring them to him. They, too, he felt, were counting the seconds until they could make a noisy escape down the hospital stairs into the street.

Only Nanny seemed natural and easy-going

and strength-giving. She settled herself solidly into the chair by the side of the bed and, clasping her large handbag, which contained practically everything, in her lap, gave herself over to scolding him.

She said, "It's the life you lead. Nobody can lead a life like that and not pay for it."

Amused, he asked her, quietly, "What do you mean by a life like that?"

But she was too shrewd to be trapped into deep waters where she could only flounder and make a spectacle of herself before a man whose business was words, and she said, "Always rushing about, seeing too many kinds of people and none of them worth anything. Oh, you know what I mean, Mr. Ashford. Don't pretend you don't. I know you well enough for that. I know the kind of upbringing you must have had. You ought to know better."

He did know what she meant, exactly, but even he, whose business was words, could not explain it more clearly than she had done. "Too

[75]

many kinds of people and none of them worth anything." The people he knew and saw were the successful, the envied, the respected; yet she was right. She was talking about values more eternal and solid than any values they knew.

"You're getting middle-aged, Mr. Ashford," she said. "It's time to settle down. Sometimes it's not so easy"—and then she gave him a faint dig out of her armory of common sense—"especially when you're used to flattery from everyone, most of all from women."

At that she began to frighten him again, and he turned off the conversation to something else. He was not yet ready to look at himself with Scottish honesty.

Presently they allowed him to see the letters which had accumulated during his illness, not the business letters at first, but only those of friends, and among these there were two from Maisie. The handwriting was a sudden shock to him because during his illness she had become a distant figure, like some woman he had loved

long ago. And the impetuous, reckless character
of the writing disturbed him and brought back
that last glimpse of her face, anguished and
frightened and very real, as the elevator slipped
downward, bearing him out of sight.

Still holding the unopened letter in his hand,
the full significance of that final scene struck
him for the first time. At the moment he had
been too numbed for it to make any impression
upon his intelligence, but now he saw the full
horror of it. Maisie, the proud, self-sufficient,
independent Maisie had abased herself shame-
lessly like the weakest of women, and he had
treated her vilely. He remembered dimly that
she had called him a monster, and now with the
unopened letter in his hand he knew that this
was true. But he knew, too, that it was over and
he was free. The letter read:

"DARLING: I didn't mean any of the
things I said last night. I didn't know
what I was doing. You're no saint, but

that's why I love you so much I made a fool of myself. You must know that's true, because you know me. And all the time I was hating you I was sorry for you. I know what it is to be tormented. Only I was so tired. I wanted to rest. That's what you wanted, too. And that I could give you and you could give me. Only you won't let it happen. What is it you're afraid of? Why won't you let people come near you? I love you. I'll love you forever. It's a terrible kind of love. I can't go on living without seeing you and hearing you and having you somewhere near me. I've never said that before to anyone. I'm not a silly schoolgirl. I ought to know love when I see it. So there you are.

MAISIE.

The letter shook him a little, but less with love

for Maisie than for himself, because somehow
she made him see himself through her eyes. It
was for a moment as if he were Maisie writing
to himself, and that brought back something of
the old confidence and recklessness. For a moment he felt a flicker of excitement. "I suppose,"
he thought, "that was really the essence of Don
Juan and Casanova. They were always making
love to themselves and so they never quite succeeded, and it went on forever." That was a
thought which two months earlier could never
have occurred to him.

The second letter read:

"DARLING: I know you're too ill to
read this now, but I know the worst
is past and that you're going to get
well. I tried to see you, but they
wouldn't let me. Sally said you
couldn't see anyone at all. I stayed on
in New York for two weeks, calling
up the house twice a week, until I

knew you were going to be all right. Then I came out here. They made an awful row about my holding up the picture, but I guess I can survive that. Go away some place now, away from all the nonsense, and have a rest. If you don't want to answer this, even if you don't ever want to see me again, I can take it. But I'll still love you just the same and I'll still want to give you a little peace, if you'd only let me. I'll write to you sometimes even if you never answer me, because that'll be a relief. And I'll love you always and always. You see, we should have met and joined up long ago before we both became so hard, because we're both adventurers. We'd understand each other. I know. We can't bear silly people who can't walk alone, and that's awful. Good-by, darling.

MAISIE.

When the nurse had gone out of the room, he lay for a long time thinking, disturbed and miserable and moved all at once. For a time, with his eyes closed, he thought of breaking it off altogether with Sally and going back to Maisie, but in the end he rejected the idea, telling himself that it was because of the two boys, who ought not suffer from a divorce. But in his heart he knew that it was because he was afraid, not of Maisie, but of the curious passion that infected the two short notes. It was more than he wanted from her or from any woman. So he told himself that it was his duty to try to patch it up again with Sally and bring some sort of order and decency into the relationship between themselves and between them and the boys. He would have to make her love him again. After all, in a few years he and Sally would be middle-aged and it would be time to give way to the boys and their right to parents who had dignity; in a way it was already time for him and Sally to stop living altogether for themselves.

So when Sally came in at teatime he took her hand and said, "Sally, I've an idea."

He felt her draw a little away from him and then pull herself together, and he thought, "If it's as bad as that, she must hate me," but he gave no sign of having noticed anything. Gravely he said, "I want us to take the boys and clear out of here as soon as I'm able to go."

She smiled, a little with relief, a little as if she were humoring a child, and said: "Of course, my dear. That's what we're going to do. I've taken passage on the *Bremen* for the first."

"Do we have to go on the *Bremen*?"

"Why not? It's the quickest. There'll be people we know. It'll be amusing."

He was silent for a moment, saying to himself: "That God-damned word 'amusing,' how I hate it." Aloud he said, "I wanted to go on a slow boat where we wouldn't see anyone we knew."

He saw that she was disappointed, but she

said, "Of course, if you think it's better for you. I hate dull boats."

"It's better for all of us. It'll be a change, and I think that's what we all need. And I want to take the boys to some quiet place where I can get acquainted with them."

"Don't talk sentimental rot." She smiled. "You know they like Antibes."

"How could they know whether they like it or not? They've never known anything else."

"Children are different nowadays and the boys are modern children. You ought to see that, if you know them at all. There's no reason why we should bore ourselves to death in some God-forsaken hole night after night after they've gone to bed. Places like that can be pretty awful. I know what they're like. I had enough of them for two summers when mamma thought she was poor."

He saw suddenly that it was going to be much more difficult than he had imagined. His own tempo was slow now, from weakness, but

Sally was still going at the same speed, that devastating speed which left time for nothing. He took her hand and said, "Sally, don't you think we might patch it up and make things go again the way they used to?" And as he spoke he was aware that what he had to have, if he was to be saved, was peace and reality.

She looked away from him and said: "They're going all right. What's the matter with them?" Her voice sounded small and hard, and for the first time it occurred to him that she was aware of how they had slipped away from each other and that it made a difference to her. But at the same time the old resentment at her shallowness took possession of him and he was filled with contempt and anger. It was no good. If he lost his temper they would get nowhere. She was a vain woman, and in the past when he had let her feel his contempt, she had always become hysterical with outraged vanity. So quietly he took her hand again and quietly he said, "We're not so young as we once were."

"You needn't rub it in."

"The time's coming when we shall have to think of middle age, and even old age, for that matter. What are we going to have, living as we do?"

She did not answer him, and he thought, "She's been thinking of marrying Malcolm."

"You don't hate me, do you?"

"No. No, I certainly don't hate you. Only, for a long time now I've felt that I don't exist at all so far as you're concerned. I used to feel it at times, long ago when we were first married. Sometimes I think nobody means anything to you. It must be horrible to be so self-sufficient."

It was odd that she should be saying the same things Maisie had said in her outburst of bitterness, and it surprised him, too, that Sally had the penetration to understand the thing she was speaking of.

"You mean I'm a monster?"

"Sometimes."

"Selfishness?"

"No, it isn't selfishness exactly. You're generous. You're good-natured. You'll compromise. You keep your temper. But all that is because you like things to go along easily and want everybody to like you. But underneath nobody exists but yourself, and in your heart you know that you're stronger than any of us, and that you'll get what you want." For a moment she was silent, thinking, and then she said: "It's very subtle and difficult to explain. It isn't really yourself. It isn't even your work. It's what you can wring from the world—success and money and admiration and love—even love. You'd like everyone to love you without its costing you anything."

"If I tried to be different would you give me a chance—for old times' sake?" But she did not answer him and he said: "I'll do my best—I promise—for your sake and the boys', and my own as well. I must. I have to. It's the only way out."

For a moment she was still and then she asked:

"What is it you want to do?"

"I want to go away to some pleasant quiet place where we won't see any clever, successful people."

She interrupted him. "Failures aren't very good company. You ought to know that, better than anyone. There's nothing worse than people eaten up with envy."

"I don't mean that we should live among failures. I suppose I'm thinking of people for whom the idea of success or failure never occurs. It's only ambitious people who are concerned with success and failure. I want to escape from ambitious people and live for a time among people who are content just to live and so find some richness in life. I used to know people like that when I was a boy. I've never known any since I came to New York. I know exactly what I mean."

"Well, I must say I don't understand. It sounds to me very dull and suburban."

It seemed to him that he could not make it any clearer save by telling her of examples, like

Eliane and her father, but since he had never spoken of them or the gray old house to her, it was too late now to explain.

"I want us to establish some sort of human relationship among ourselves—you and I and the boys. I want us to be a family."

And then, astonishingly, she said, "I'd like that, I think, more than anything," and when she said that the plan suddenly came very clear to his mind, as if it had been there all the time and needed only a word to be born. It came rushing from him, eloquently, far more eloquently than if he had prepared a whole speech in advance, and while he was talking he knew that, without knowing it, this was what he had wanted for a long time. It was this which had come between himself and Maisie and produced in him that strange hypnotizing numbness which had dampened all his feeling for her.

He found himself telling her about the house and the garden that ran down to the river. He

[88]

told her nothing of Eliane or of her father, but only described the place with its curious still sense of beauty and eternity. He told her that it was a place he had known well during the war and that he had lived there for a long time after he was wounded. The place might be for sale or for rent, and even if it wasn't he could have it by paying through the nose.

"We've always done that, anyway," he said, "about anything we've wanted. If it worked out and we found contentment there, it would be worth anything. We could live there and send the boys to school in England, and I could write the kind of plays I've never written, instead of the kind that are simply successful because I know the trick better than the next fellow. It's so damned easy to be successful—so damned easy."

When he had finished he discovered that she was crying and it occurred to him that, after all, if he made the least effort, he could win her back from Malcolm, who had no eloquence, no fire, and no words. He took her hand and said, "Will you try it, darling?"

"I don't know," she said. "Give me until to-morrow. I don't want to be a fool."

He knew then that she wanted to talk it over with Malcolm before deciding, but suddenly he had no fear of Malcolm.

The next afternoon she told him that she had thought it all over and decided to try it. And for that he knew that he had to thank Malcolm, who was a good, dull, stupid fellow. If he had been in Malcolm's place, he wouldn't have given Sally's husband a second thought.

When she had gone he took Maisie's two letters from the book in which he had concealed them and, tearing them into small bits, threw them into the waste-paper basket. The gesture gave him a feeling of decision and virtue, of which he was immediately ashamed.

Part Two

Part Two

HE SAW THE GARDEN FOR THE FIRST TIME EIGHT
days before the Armistice was signed, when,
opening his eyes, he found himself in a big low
room which he had never seen before. There
were wide tall windows which opened outward
into the autumn sunlight, and on the sill of one
of them, its white paws curled beneath its chest,
slept a tortoise-shell cat. At first he felt very

tired and lay for a little time with his eyes closed, and presently the sense of bewilderment left him, its place taken by curiosity, and pulling himself up a little in the bed, he looked out of the window. What he saw was a wide stretch of unkempt lawn strewn with the dying leaves of the plane trees, and beyond a little river and a marsh bordered with flags and pools of water here and there which were the deep blue of lapis lazuli. Beyond lay the crisp gold-and-red line of a beech forest. In the midst of the marsh, on a little island with a bridge leading to it, stood a tiny belvedere, white and simple in the classic style of the eighteenth century.

At the far end of the room there was a stone fireplace, and a little nearer a great wardrobe of carved wood and a few old chairs on which the upholstery had grown a little shabby, and near at hand, beside him on a little table, stood a pitcher of water and a glass and a small blue bowl filled with aster and Michaelmas daisies. There was a strange profound sense of peace and stillness, broken only by the chirping of the sparrows on the lawn.

In the beginning, confused and weak, it occurred to him that perhaps he had died and gone to heaven, because at that time heaven seemed to him simply a place where there was peace and stillness and clean white sheets and a comfortable bed. And it was still, so still in all that sunlight that you could hear the rustle of the dead leaves stirred by the breeze. And the bed was unmistakably a real bed, enormous, high, soft, and clean, and a trifle short for his six feet two of length. It was the bandage and the faint dull ache in his head, which gave him the first clue as to what had happened to him. Where and how he had been wounded he did not know, for the last thing he remembered was standing in the *promenoir* of the Casino de Paris between an English soldier and a French one, watching Mistinguette. Slowly and with a great effort he pushed his memory a little farther, until he knew that after that he had left

Paris on his motorcycle, meaning to be in St. Quentin by daylight.

He remembered passing the gates and being stopped, and showing his papers as a dispatch rider and then very little more until he crossed railway tracks somewhere on the edge of a town where suddenly there was a terrific explosion quite near at hand which had thrown him off the motorcycle into a ditch. Vaguely and with an effort he remembered having picked himself up. There was a warm, wet sensation on the side of his face and he found that blood was coming from a great cut on his head. He remembered dimly having torn up his shirt to bandage his head and having climbed back again on the motorcycle, thinking, "I have to be at St. Quentin by daylight." The bomb must have been dropped by a plane which he did not hear above the roaring of his own motorcycle.

And now, miraculously, he was here in this big cool room instead of being in an army hospital with rows of men in cots on either side.

How he came here or why he had not been taken away, he could not fathom. Still wondering, he closed his eyes to shut away the autumn sunlight from the ache in his head, and presently he fell asleep.

When he wakened it was evening, and as he opened his eyes he was aware that he was not alone in the room. Between him and the window where the cat had been sleeping in the sunlight there was the figure of a woman. And in the dim light he could see that she was dressed in black and that she was young. She carried a bowl and a spoon in her hand, and before he was able to discern her features she said, *"Bon jour, mon ami,"* in a low voice of great beauty and softness.

To his *"Bon jour"* she responded, to his surprise, in English. "I'm glad you're feeling better. I've brought you some consommé."

Then she put down the bowl and lighted a lamp, which she placed on the table at the foot of his bed, and by the dim light he saw that she

[97]

was dark, with dark eyes and small, beautiful hands. She was young, not, he guessed, more than his own age. And she had fine black brows which nearly met across the bridge of her nose, and her mouth was full and curled a little at the corners, as if she always found life pleasant and amusing in spite of everything. Long afterward when she had vanished, he always remembered her expression as he had first seen her. It was the face of one who was not afraid of life and knew how to deal with it.

Painfully he raised himself a little in the bed and noticed for the first time that he was wearing an old-fashioned nightgown, too small for him, with a design embroidered in red cotton thread. She came close to the bed, and when he moved as if to take the bowl from her, she said: "No. You're not strong enough. I'll give it to you. It'll be much easier that way." And seating herself beside him, she fed him the broth spoonful by spoonful.

While he ate she talked to him, saying:

"You'll be better in a few days. You had a dislocated shoulder and concussion and you lost a lot of blood."

When he had finished eating she smoothed the pillows and picked up the bowl again, but he said, "Don't go away, please. Tell me where I am and how I got here."

She smiled at him and into her eyes came a friendly look of mischief, as if she understood that what had happened was all very extraordinary and romantic, but that neither of them must take it too seriously or begin to act like characters in a romantic story. "My name is Mademoiselle Eliane Vainville, born in England twenty years ago. This house belongs to my father. We found you outside the lower garden gate four days ago. What happened? Where had you come from?"

He told her what he could remember about the bomb and the railroad crossing and picking himself up, and after a moment she said, "That must have happened at Buzancy. The Boches bombed Buzancy that night. What I don't see is how you got as far as this. Buzancy is ten kilometers from here."

"I only remember thinking that I had to be in St. Quentin by daylight. I guess I must have tried to make it."

Then she told him that Louise, the servant, had found him and his motorcycle both smashed up against the gate. With the help of the old gardener they had carried him in. "Your motor-cycle is in the stable. I think it can be repaired. It looks like a very beautiful powerful motor-cycle. It would be a pity if it's spoiled."

So they had put him to bed and she herself had gone to the nearest village to fetch Doctor Pressard, who was home on leave from his regi-ment, and Doctor Pressard came every day to care for him. "He had to go back to his regi-ment yesterday, but he said everything would be all right if you were quiet and careful for a time. He said you must rest here for at least two weeks."

Then he wondered what they would think at headquarters—probably that he had overstayed in Paris to enjoy himself. For a moment it worried him and then suddenly he was too tired to care. And in the peace and luxury of his surroundings the troubles faded into nothing.

"Does anyone know I'm here?" he asked.

"Nobody but Doctor Pressard and one or two people in the village."

"I ought to send word to my colonel."

She smiled. "Don't worry about that. In a day or two they won't need you and nobody will care whether you come back or not. It's almost over. The *Temps* says a day or two more. They wouldn't need you even if you were able to come back." She picked up the bowl. "I'm going to leave you. Doctor Pressard says you must have quiet and not excite yourself."

But he had to ask one more question, "How do you speak English so well?"

She laughed. "I've lived in England half my

life. You see, my father is a radical politician and sometimes he couldn't live in France unless he wanted to go to prison, so we went to England—like Voltaire." She gave the pillow another pat and from her body came the clean cool scent of the lemon verbena in which her clothes were kept. For a moment he thought of Aunt Cassie and her Sunday black clothes which always smelled of lavender.

"I'll leave you the night lamp," she said, "and then you must try to go to sleep. If you want anything, ring the bell beside your bed."

To leave the room she had to walk the whole length to the far end, and lying back on his pillow he watched her until she went out, leaving the door open behind her. It gave into a hallway floored with red tiling. The room was quite dark now except for the small circle of light from the lamp. It struck him that there was something extraordinarily soothing and calm about her. She was cheerful and she did not make him feel shy. She moved with a quiet assurance, never fumbling, and as she walked she set her feet down proudly and lightly rather like a bird. The faint scent of lemon verbena returned to him and he closed his eyes, voluptuously conscious of the cool clean sheets and the soft pillow.

It had been a long time since he had seen any woman save peasants and the girls who walked the dark sidewalks of Paris and frequented the *promenoirs* of the music-halls, plucking at him and making obscene gestures, and now the sight of this girl, so like and yet so different from the girls he had known through all his boyhood, stirred him, arousing his curiosity and stimulating his imagination. Long afterward, whenever he thought of that moment of coming back to life as he saw her moving across the room in the twilight, he felt a sharp stinging sensation in his eyes as if he could weep, not only over having lost her forever, but over himself, lying there in the clean fresh bed, so young and so romantic, so clean and so determined that life should be fine and beautiful; because none of those women, either in the *promenoirs* or in the brothels where he sometimes went to drink, had ever touched him at all. In his virginity they had seemed to him coarse and pitiful and shocking. For he was born and trained an idealist and a romantic; Aunt Cassie and all his Middle Western childhood had made it so.

With the fever still burning in his head, this girl, crossing the room was above all else cool and clean, like a flower in the early morning before the dew has been burnt from it. Without thinking of it, the sight of her sent his mind back years and years over all the mornings when he had risen a little after dawn to find the dew still glittering on the spider webs in the vegetable garden and the bobolinks singing in the fields of timothy. Afterward he knew, too, that it was inevitable that he should fall in love with her. Waking alone in a strange house in cleanliness and comfort, he would have fallen in love at once with almost any woman who cared for his weary, broken body and spirit. His luck had been to waken and find Eliane.

Vaguely he thought, "She is lovely—not just pretty, but something more than that." What it was he could not quite discover at the moment, but after he had lost her and he grew older he came to understand the meaning of that quality. With his eyes closed, he wondered what it would be like to love and be loved, to waken in the morning with a girl like that beside you. What he dreamed of was an impossible love, detached from life and reality, a kind of romantic enchantment which went on and on and had nothing to do with bread and clothes and a roof over your head. He dreamed of passion and tenderness and humor and of all those things which he had always believed should be a part of one's first encounter with a woman.

And then hearing a faint sound, he opened his eyes and there she was again in the room, walking toward him in the same delicate way, carrying a little porcelain teapot in one hand

[105]

and a candle in the other. The faint light of the candle was thrown upward on her face, bringing out the fine modeling of the cheek bones and the temples. The teapot stood on a little stand of white porcelain, and under it burned the flame of an alcohol lamp. She put it down on the table beside him and said: "I didn't waken you, did I? You weren't asleep?"

"No."

"I thought maybe you might not sleep well. Sometimes that happens. So I brought you some mint tea. I think I'll sleep in my own room to-night. If you need me you can always ring the bell. I'll hear it."

Until now he hadn't thought of her sleeping there night after night on the sofa in the same room with him, and now suddenly he wanted to say to her: "Don't leave me. Don't go to your own room," but he was too shy, and all he said was, "You've been very good to me."

She laughed. "It's been fun, like a game. Sometimes I get bored here, living all alone with father. There hasn't been much fun these last four years. I haven't seen anybody young for so long."

She arranged the tray beside him and then, pausing before she went out, she stood looking down at him, smiling. In her eyes there was a look which took his breath away—a pleasant, intimate look which said: "I think we're going to be friends. I like you." And in a panic it occurred to him how much better she knew him than he knew her, and he wondered what he had said and what he had done in those long hours of unconsciousness and delirium. No woman had ever looked at him like that before, so honestly and simply. Always they had been shy or coquettish or simply regarded him with a kind of physical greed because he was so young and big and innocent. It was as if she took his own shyness from him and, neatly folding it up, placed it where he could never find it again.

When she had gone he had a strange feeling that between them there was something destined by fate, not knowing then that lovers always think such things. It seemed to him that he had been here before in some other life, in this same old room with the cat asleep on the sill, and the marshes beyond; and she had been there, too. And he was happy because the loneliness he had known ever since Aunt Cassie died was suddenly gone. It was a loneliness and hunger born of a desire for the company and the touch of a woman. With men it was all right; they all liked him; he always had plenty of friends. But there had never been any women.

The next day he was worse again and a little delirious, and then two days more and suddenly the fever went away and he was quite well save for the soreness in his shoulder. When he asked for his clothes, Eliane brought in his stained ill-fitting khaki, but in spite of all her efforts to clean the uniform, nothing had been able to remove the traces of blood and oil. She said: "I have a better plan. I went to the village yes-

terday and bought some clothes, just plain workingman's clothes. They won't fit very well, but
they'll be more comfortable than these dirty old
things."

The clothes were comfortable, just blue trousers and a kind of smock of blue denim, and
when he had put them on he stood before the
glass for a long time, regarding himself and
grinning, amused and pleased. They became him
as such clothes become any man, and they seemed
somehow to have changed him. It was as if he
had risen from bed a different person. Something had been sloughed off. What it was he
could not say, but he felt the freedom of a person changed by disguise. No longer was he simply a soldier clad in rough, hideously ugly, ill-
fitting filthy tunic; a mere number might be
crushed out without anyone's missing him or
taking any notice. He was a new man now, with
individuality, with independence, with a soul
and a spirit. And the clothes made him feel a
part of the lovely landscape outside the window.

They brought to him a warm sense of belonging there. They brought him close to the good earth and somehow destroyed the last traces of his shyness. In his own clothes he would have felt strange and awkward and alien; but in the soft blue cotton trousers and smock he was some one else. It was like playing a part, a romantic part, which cut him off sharply from the world not only of the army and the war, but even from his own boyhood. Not one person out of the life he had lived before knew where he was or what had become of him. It was like having died and come to life again in a new world.

When he came out she was waiting for him in the garden, and at sight of him she laughed and said: "It's perfect. You look exactly right. If anyone saw you on the road they'd think you were a Norman farmer on your way home from driving your cattle to market. You look like a Norman—big and blond. When you get your color back nobody could tell you from one."

She told him that her mother, dead since her birth, had come from Normandy, from a great farm not far from Rouen. She said, "Let's make the tour of the property and then I'll come back and introduce you to my father."

It was a fine crisp morning with the northern sun spreading long shadows on the grass and turning the withered fallen leaves of the plane trees to gold. For the first time he saw the façade of the old house, faded gray and pale yellow and half covered by ampelopsis which had turned to scarlet and purple. The old part she told him, was built by a wine-grower in the seventeenth century, but for a hundred years or more there had been no wine-making in the Valois; the climate had changed, so the peasants said, and the grapes no longer ripened properly. The new part had been built in the eighteenth century by a banker from Paris, who had used it for a lodge when he came to shoot the deer which haunted the forest on the opposite side of the marshes. But the new part and the old had been drawn together long since by the tendrils and leaves and rootlets of wistaria and ampelopsis, so that there was an enchanting harmony, spaced with small worn plaques and high windows which opened outward into the garden.

Against the house, facing south, there was a flat terrace of gravel bordered by a stone railing and a dozen stone urns worn by the weather and splotched with golden lichen. A path ran from the house down to the edge of the river, where there was a small boat and a little arched bridge which led to the island crowned by the summer-house. Beyond, the marshes stretched out lush and green as far as the forest, which made a wall of gray beech trunks beneath a canopy of dying russet leaves.

At the back of the house lay the stables and a big vegetable-garden walled and protected with paths bordered by trimmed box and grapes growing against the ancient stone. On each side of the paths were planted rows of tiny apple and pear trees carefully pruned and burdened with fruit. It had been a good year for fruit, she said, warm and dry and sunny. It wasn't often like that here in the Valois.

In front of the stables, in a small walled court with a gate opening into the garden, they met an old woman called Louise coming out with a pail of warm frothy milk, fresh from the cow. She was aged and bent with a lined cheery face, and at sight of them she grinned. She had not a single tooth.

"This is Louise," said Eliane. "She helped me to look after you when you were unconscious."

The old woman put down the pail, wiped her ancient hands on her apron, and shook his hand, peasant fashion, saying in French that she was delighted that monsieur was well again and could walk about.

"We thought," she said, with a kind of morbid pleasure, "that we were going to lose you. When we found you outside on the road, with your head all broken and everything, I said to myself 'Here's another fine fellow lost to the

[113]

world'; but it's all come out all right." She beamed at him toothlessly and Tom's heart warmed to her simplicity and benevolence and dignity. She had a new quality, different from the quality of democracy in his own country. Every gesture and intonation said, "I am a woman without ambition save for peace and security. I am content to fill my small niche in life conscientiously and well." There was neither restlessness nor discontent in the lined old face.

She picked up her pail and moved off toward the house. "She's been with my father," said Eliane, "since before I was born. When he had to go to England she stayed behind to care for the place. She's the only servant we have, except old Picquet who looks after the garden. Between us we looked after you. You'll never get away from her now. She thinks you belong to her. You must write to her when you go away. You're her discovery. She found you when she opened the gate."

"I must have made a lot of work."

Eliane smiled. "No. I told you it was fun for both of us. And we're proud, too, because we saved a fine healthy young man who might have died otherwise. We cheated the war of one more. There have been so many killed—forty-three from out our little village." Her face became grave and the light went suddenly out of her dark eyes. "Sometimes I wake up in the night and think there won't be any *young* men left in the world when this war is finished. I ought to be married by now and having a family, but who am I to marry?"

He looked at her sharply and saw at once that she wasn't thinking of him as a husband. "That's why," she continued, "it was so nice of you to break your head right on our doorstep. It gave me a *young* man to care for, a little while, anyway."

They walked back through what had once been a flower-garden where everything had gone wild because old Picquet couldn't manage both flowers and vegetables, and so the flowers had had to be sacrificed. Nothing had survived except the hardiest of plants and the corners were filled now with tufts of russet and gold chrysanthemums. At the edge of the path Eliane suddenly stopped and bent down. "Look," she said. "The first buds on the Christmas roses." He looked, and far down among the sturdy deep green leaves he saw tiny clusters of round tight little buds the color of pomegranate. He had never seen Christmas roses before. "When the buds open," she said, "the flowers will be white and waxy like camellias."

The gesture touched him in an odd way and filled him with a sudden nostalgia for the place where he was born. He understood that Eliane felt about this place the way he felt about the farm. She knew every plant and she watched them from day to day, visiting them to see them bud and flower and set their seeds. She felt as he did about the earth and everything that grew on it. She knew that even weeds were magical and wonderful things, full of beauty. She knew this place as he knew the farm, every stick and stone and tree. It was her whole world, and once the gate was closed she was as content in that world as he had been on the farm, save in those moments of wild restlessness when ambition and curiosity filled him with a kind of madness and it seemed to him that he would suffocate if he did not escape and see and conquer the world beyond the line fence.

But Aunt Cassie was dead and her daughter was selling the farm, and probably he would never see it again.

They crossed the little bridge to the Palladian summer-house and here they sat for a time because he felt suddenly weak and dizzy. It was as if they were seated in a ship. On one side of the river stood the forest all gray and gold, the ground underneath mottled with blue shadows, and on the other side stood the house, gray and gold, too, save for the bold splash of the scarlet and purple ampelopsis. He thought suddenly,

[117]

"How wonderful it would be to stay here forever shut off from the world," but at the same time he knew that he felt thus only because he was ill and weak and very tired of filth and noise and vileness. As soon as his strength returned the old restlessness and ambition would come back, too.

"We sit here sometimes in the evening," she was saying. "The light is beautiful—as beautiful as the light in Spain, but different—it is blue here instead of violet—and sometimes the sunsets are glorious."

"You've been a lot of places," he said.

"Yes. I always went with my father. I've been to Austria and Spain and England and Germany, when I was a little girl, but I like this best. I'm always glad to come back. I don't like hotels and strange houses. I've always lived here when we were able to. I'm like a plant, I suppose. This is where my roots are. Sometimes when I was away from here, I used to dream that I was a plant in the vegetable-garden and that my roots went down and down until they reached the water that seeps in from the river and makes our vegetables so fine. It was cool and damp." She laughed. "It was funny. In my dreams I could feel it. It was like having a drink of cold clear water on a hot day."

He knew what she meant. The water in the river all about them was cold and clear as crystal, and above the green weeds that twisted in the current you could see the gudgeons swimming about so plainly that you could almost count their scales. It was a homesickness not for any person, but for a place itself, for the very earth, the familiar brooks and valley, the stables where the animals spoke to you when you opened the stable doors, for the old spring house with the milk and butter chilled by the icy water that bubbled up from among the stones.

He was too tired to talk much and presently he was aware that she was looking at him, and he turned to meet her eyes. There was a smile in them and that same frankness and simplicity

he had encountered before. He grinned and said,
"Do I look very funny in these clothes?"

"No. I don't think you look funny at all. You
look very handsome and very right and you look
as if they belonged to you and you to them. Anyway, the clothes of a workingman always have
dignity no matter how old and worn they are.
They are never ridiculous the way the clothes of
a pompous bourgeois so often are. But I wasn't
thinking of that. I was thinking how funny it
was that you and I should be sitting here together . . . you who come from a different part
of the world, from people who are so different.
It's very exciting. I keep wondering what your
family and your house must be like and what
you're really thinking. That's the most important
of all. I've traveled lots, a million times more
than most French people, and sometimes when
I'm alone here I've wanted to set out again
traveling. I'd like to see the whole world." She
sighed suddenly. "But I never will. My father
is finished with traveling and when he's dead,

I shan't ever go anywhere." Then she rose and said, "Let's go back now. I think my father will be up and dressed. He's been wanting to see you."

"Hasn't he seen me, even while I was unconscious?"

"No. You see, he's very old and ill. He was sixty-five years old when I was born. He can't get about much. He usually stays in his chair all day."

They recrossed the bridge and went to the end of the house nearest the stable, where she led him into a big high room which must once have been a great salon for parties. Long since, it had been converted into a kind of study for the old gentleman, her father. There he sat at the far end of the room in a kind of smaller nest made of newspapers he had read and thrown on the floor all about him. He was a tiny, withered old man, like a mouse with a pair of black gimlet eyes. They were the first thing one saw. Tom was aware of them the whole length of the big

[121]

room. The sun came in the big windows, bath-
ing the old gentleman with light.

Long afterward, when the old man was dead
and Eliane had disappeared, Tom discovered
how powerful and important was this little
mouse with the bright eyes, but as he came in
the door, a big awkward boy fresh from the
Middle West, the name of Vainville meant
nothing to him. He did not know that the little
mouse was one of those who had gnawed for
half a century at the foundations of a whole
civilization built upon cruelty and injustice, hy-
pocrisy and privilege. He only knew that in the
bright eyes and the withered little body there
was a strange fire which impressed and frightened him. He had never before met a great man
and never before met a man who had sacrificed
wealth and ambition and success for the sake
of an ideal.

The little mouse rose from his big chair and,
holding to the edge of the table for support, held
out a tiny hand.

"Good morning, sir," he said in excellent English. "I'm delighted to see you. It was good luck that dumped you off in front of our gate. It brought company for Eliane and if you'd gone to St. Quentin you might have been dead by now." He looked Tom over quite frankly, from head to foot, so that the boy blushed with self-consciousness, aware that somehow those black gimlet eyes were seeing quite through him. "Yes," he said, "fine figure of a fellow. That blouse becomes you. It becomes anyone better than a uniform."

Tom made a halting awkward speech of gratitude, at which the old man laughed. "You'll have to stay here until you're quite well."

"I must get back to my regiment."

"There's no hurry about that. I've got news for you. It's fresh from Paris from some one who should know. It'll all be finished about this time tomorrow—the actual fighting will be finished, but the war will go on and on long after even you and Eliane are in your graves."

The old gentleman sat down and asked Tom questions about America and about himself. He talked about the war in a way which was puzzling to Tom, not as if it were the only thing which existed in the world, but as if it were an incident, one of importance, to be sure, but one which was simply a link in a whole chain of events which he viewed from a great distance instead of from near at hand; and while Tom listened it seemed to him that in the presence of the old gentleman he himself grew smaller and smaller, younger and younger. He was like a little child. He learned, too, that for the old man, as for his daughter, this world of this house and garden was the reality to which they returned from time to time out of a stormy world which was only folly, confusion, and noise. It was here the old gentleman returned to rest after battle. This house and garden with the forest beyond was a whole world, a kind of refuge in which there was eternal peace. One need never go outside it, for it was paradise itself. Eve was there, but there was no Adam unless Adam was himself.

He was too young then and too empty of experience to know the power of his own physical charm and of that vitality which persisted even through illness and shock and pain, and so it never occurred to him that the daughter of the gentlemanly old mouse might fall in love with him. In his modesty and naïveté, he never dreamed of using these weapons to gain what in his heart he had wanted since the beginning. Years later he learned all the tricks, coming to know that with certain women he could do as he liked. He learned that it was possible to turn on both charm and flattery as from a tap, but during those weeks in the old house and garden, it never occurred to him to cheapen what God and nature had given him, and so he was at first simply young and timid and toward the end ardent and tormented.

During all those weeks the old gentleman took

[125]

little notice of them save sometimes in the morning when they went in to see him in the big room littered with books and newspapers. He never knew whether the old man was aware of what was happening, for he never gave any hint save once, when they were sitting with him in the sunshine on the terrace and he said, "I've taught Eliane many things, but most of all to be able to care for herself. I believe women should be taught to live like men, but I did it for her especially because I was so old when she was born." And then Tom discovered that the girl was an expert horticulturist and that she could, if necessary, make her living in a half-dozen other ways. "No one knows," said the old mouse, "what is ahead. We're tearing down everything to make way for a new world, and in that new world women must look out for themselves and make their own decisions." And then he chuckled a little wickedly, as he always did when he regarded the prospect of a capitalist world wrecking itself by trickeries and dishonesty and wars. "They made this war," he would say, "hoping for gain, and so they helped us. It will only destroy them in the end."

In the whole garden there was no one to interfere with them, to mock or to make jealousies or intrigues. In that Eden there was no serpent. Even old Louise and the gardener Picquet watched them from a distance, smiling benevolently and thinking perhaps of their own youth and of how fine life had been when they were young and strong and love was still a reality. With a hypocritical look of detachment and innocence, old Louise one morning even remarked to Eliane that her first lover had been a soldier in the Franco-Prussian war.

When he grew a little stronger he helped Eliane with the vegetable-garden, wondering at the strength of her slight body and at the skill with which she handled the tender plants and did the pruning. She had the touch of the earth. He knew it because himself had it. Only those who had it were proper gardeners. For others

[127]

plants died and seeds withered in the ground. Eliane was one of those who brought fertility wherever she went. In the morning and evening he milked the two cows and turned them out in the green pasture beside the river. He helped Eliane in the kitchen. It was all very like the life of his childhood, save that this place was more still and beautiful and there was about it a quality of eternity which the houses and barns and even the people of his own world somehow never attained. Slowly he became aware of the presence there in the garden of all those who had loved and cherished this spot since before history began. They were still there in every stone, in every tile, in every tree and vine. This house and garden with the still peace which hung over them were the creation of generations of men and women who had loved the spot and the very earth itself.

They worked and lived thus for day after day, in sunlight and rain, and in the evenings, dressed warmly, they sometimes sat in the little white belvedere on the island while the blue evening light seemed to sift down like powder among the trees of the forest and over the ancient house, and when it was dark they went into the house and themselves cooked a supper which they ate at the table in the huge kitchen with the copper pots and pans shining against the wall all about them in the firelight.

Then it was that he discovered she was an excellent cook. It amused her to show him all the things she could do—dishes of beef and veal and carrots and beans, both haricots and flageo-lets, and cabbage, and a dozen kinds of ome-lettes. And from her he learned how wines should be treated and how one kind of wine was right with one sort of dish and wrong with another. He learned things about food and drink which, because he was by nature sensual, he never forgot for the rest of his life. Beneath the house, so deep and so well hidden that even the Germans had not found it when they came there three years before, there was a cellar built three hundred years earlier by the wine-grower who had first lived in the house and there covered with mold lay bottle upon bottle of wine which had been put away conscientiously year after year by the little old mouse to ripen slowly into nectar.

She told him about herself, admitting that there was not much to tell. It was himself who did most of the talking, for she wanted to know everything about his life in America, and while she listened, he himself grew more confident and expansive. He told her about the farm in the Middle West and of his great ambitions to become famous and successful and in the end to conquer the world itself and come to know London and Paris and New York as well as he knew the place back in Illinois. He talked with his eyes shining, and at the light in them she smiled too, her lips curling a little at the corners, so that suddenly he would become abruptly silent, as if she were mocking his enthusiasm out of an experience longer and more profound than she could ever have acquired during her twenty years of living.

Once while he was talking thus she looked at him in astonishment and said: "But the land. Are you giving it up forever?"

He tried to explain to her that there was so much to see and so much to do that he could not even think about that for years.

"But you love it, don't you? I know you do. I can see it."

"Yes, but I can't be buried there all my life when there's so much outside in the world."

She extinguished her cigarette and looked at him across the table, her eyes dark with serious-ness and concentration. "I see," she said, quietly. "Of course I see."

Sometimes on sunny afternoons they rowed across the river and walked through the forest. Sometimes they surprised a stag and his harem, and now and then on the edge of the fields they started up pheasants. In the evening when they returned, the pasture by the river would be dotted with rabbits which had come out at sunset. Mostly they walked to an open space in the forest where the earth turned to sand and only birch trees and scrub pines and heather could find enough goodness to live upon, and there in a great hollow of golden sand they would lie in the sun, sometimes speaking, sometimes silent, listening to the sounds of the forest all about them.

Then it was that he grew troubled and while his face grew hot with the stifled desire to reach over and take her body to his, he would hold on himself and repeat all the arguments which he used to hold himself in check. He would say to himself that he could not behave thus toward the daughter of a man who had taken him off the road into his house. He could not do it when it was impossible to think of offering marriage, when he was without money, without a home, without even a job. One afternoon when the pain became unbearable he said to himself: "I must go away tomorrow. It is the only thing left to do." Rising abruptly, he said: "Come. It's late. We must go back." But she did not stir. She covered her face with her hands and was silent, and presently he said, "I shall have to go away tomorrow." And at that she looked up at him and said, "Sit here, beside me, while I talk to you." Then without looking at him she sat up and said in a low voice: "You mustn't say that. You mustn't go away—not yet." Then her face grew thoughtful and she said, "You see, it isn't finished yet. It isn't complete. Things have to be complete or life means nothing."

He took her hand and kissed it and then suddenly it was as if there had been a great explosion and all the world around them had been blown to bits and nothing of it remained. There were waves of light, brilliant and magnificent. His whole body became lighter than the shining air, and they were no longer alone and separated, but one superb and shining entity. And

then presently they were still with a profound
and shining peace all about them and inside
them. Her head rested against his face and in
awe he found himself with his eyes closed, thinking, "We should die now. We should not go on
living."

After a little while he kissed her and said,
softly, "What have I done? What have I done?"
And opening hers, she looked up at him and
smiled. "You've done what I wanted. You've
done what had to be done. It's what matters
most in life." And suddenly all that was Puritan
in him, all that was bound and twisted and
crooked, all that had come out of a life which
besides hers was crude and stifled and bare of
wisdom was gone and he thought: "Now I am
alive. Now I can live. I will never again be
afraid, not even of death." And even then,
young as he was and without knowledge, he felt
arrogant and proud because he knew that he
was more fortunate than other men. Somehow
he understood deep inside himself that he

had known what few of them would ever know.

That night after he had gone to bed he lay awake, sleepless with an excitement stronger than anything he had ever known before, listening to the sounds of the old house—the scurry of mice deep within the ancient walls, the faint creaking of the old chairs as the heat melted slowly from the room, and now and then out of the midst of other faint sounds he discerned what seemed to be the distant sound of footsteps and his heart beat faster, not from fear, but in the hope that it was Eliane coming to him. There was no longer any shyness or any scruples; there was only love and the necessity of going on and on with something which must be fulfilled or he would never again live in peace. Again and again he listened to the faint sounds, never knowing whether they existed in reality or were born out of his hope and imagination. And presently, after hours of waiting, the footsteps did not die away, but came nearer and nearer along the passageway until they reached the door. It opened slowly and Eliane came in. She was carrying a candle, and as she closed the door she blew out the flame. He was aware then of what he had known all along—that she meant to come to him. He knew that it had to be. All that night they passed in love and the next day they spent in the beechwood among the deer and the pheasants like a pair enchanted, and none interrupted them, neither the old mouse, so ancient and wise, nor old Louise dreaming of her own youth, nor Picquet the gardener.

And so he stayed on and on. Loving each other and being young, they asked nothing of the world but love, and all that went on in the world beyond the walls of the car, all the tragic celebrations, the confusions, the intrigues, the hate and the folly counted for nothing. Sometimes in their love they were like one person, and then sometimes for hours they would be alone, each of them, separated tragically from the other by things which they were too young to comprehend. But in the nights there was peace and beauty and splendor.

And then slowly the dazzling light began to fade a little. She would escape from him, never in body, but sometimes in spirit. She would be beside him and yet in some mysterious way not there at all. Whenever he spoke of the world outside or of what he planned to do, she would turn cold and mysteriously her spirit would slip away from him, leaving him miserable. There were times when he felt a wild jealousy of the very garden, that it claimed her time, that she loved it so profoundly. At moments it seemed to him that he was not her lover at all, but only an instrument of the earth itself which she loved above all else. They never spoke of marriage or of the future or of what was to happen when the day came when he must leave her and go away. Dimly he felt that she was infinitely the older and wiser and that these things must be left to her. Afterward, when he had gone, he came to see her as a symbol of that ancient place, just as he was a symbol of that farm in the Middle West where he had spent all his childhood—a farm which was beside the ancient grayness of the house and garden no more than a child.

Three days after Christmas she said to him, "I think it's time you went back to the regiment, Tom." And a little frightened, he asked, "Are you tired of me?"

She gave him a long still look and said: "No. I should never be tired of you. But it's time we took hold of life and managed things."

"That means I shall have to go back to America."

She looked at him in astonishment. "But you must have known that all along."

"I kept myself from thinking of it."

She sighed. "But that's no good. There's no good in not facing things. You see you're an adventurer and greedy. And I'm not. I have to

[138]

think of things like that. Some one has to. You can't ignore the foundations of a house."

For a long time he was silent and miserable and then he said: "But you'll come with me. We'll be married and live over there."

"I can't come with you, even if I could leave my father. Anyway, it would be silly. I couldn't ruin everything for you right at the start. You haven't a job. You haven't anything. You've got to build everything. When it's built we can talk about that." She took his hand suddenly and kissed it passionately. "Do you think I want you to go? It's like taking my heart out."

"I'll make a fortune quickly and then we'll be married."

"Yes. That's it. We'll be married." But she looked away from him and he felt a slow chill slipping over his whole body, from his heart through all his limbs. She was escaping from him again to a great distance from which he could never recapture her.

And so one morning he said good-by to all of

them—to Eliane and the sharp-eyed old mouse, Louise and the gardener Picquet, and vanished down, at last, the road through the forest on his motorcycle.

After three days he found his regiment, and when he returned they put him into the guardhouse, but he was at once so miserable and so exalted that it did not matter to him, and when they saw the blood stains on his tunic and the scar on the side of his head they believed his story at last and let him go free, because then the war had been over for only a little time and men still believed that miraculously the world would be once more as it had been before the desolation, and so everyone must be happy and forgiven.

But almost at once he discovered that the regiment was to be sent home and he was seized with a feeling of desperation, and one night at sunset he took his motorcycle and without asking leave crossed half of France, taking lanes and bypaths so he would not have to go through Paris, and at last, late the next day he arrived before the gate where old Louise had found him. It was the old woman who answered the jangling bell and let him in.

She grinned at him a toothless grin and said, "I knew you would come back, my child."

He found Eliane in the sitting-room, alone before the fire. She was sewing, and when he opened the door she turned and, seeing him, gave a faint cry and met him halfway across the room. For a long time they stayed there clinging to each other, trying to still their hunger, Eliane sobbing, pressing her face against his throat. As long as he lived he remembered the moment, for it, together with that sudden blaze of light in the sandpit, were destined to haunt him for the rest of his life, making all other loves and all other women seem meagre and colorless.

They spent the whole night in love and breathless talk, never sleeping at all, and in the morning before it was yet light she rose and made him *café au lait* and cooked eggs in the old kitchen, and then came to stand in the gateway, waving to him until the motorcycle bearing him away disappeared into the beech forest.

It was the last time he saw her.

During those first months when he was alone and friendless in New York he wrote her long letters each night, sometimes on the typewriter in the city room of the newspaper where he found a job, sometimes in the mornings in the attic room of a boarding-house where he lived on Lexington Avenue. At first, still dazed by what had happened to him, loneliness did not occur to him. In all his young world there existed only himself and Eliane; all the others were shadows. He wrote her of what happened to him and what he thought and of the plans he had for them both when he made enough money for her to come to America.

At first she, too, wrote every day, but for her there was much less to write; there was only the

news of the village and of Louise and the cows
and the old gardener, and then one day she
wrote that when she went in to wake her father
in the morning she had found him dead. At that
he wrote at once that she must waste no time,
but come to him immediately; he had a job
which paid him twenty-five dollars a week and
she was free. But she did not come. Instead, he
had from her a practical letter in which she
translated dollars into francs and showed him
how absurd the idea was and how unfair it
would be for her to ruin his hopes at the very
beginning, by creating a burden which would
sap his freedom forever.

"I know your ambitions," she wrote. "They
are stronger than you think."

And in his heart he knew that she was right,
for slowly the city had begun to open before
him, an enchanted place where one could have
what one wanted if the desire were only strong
enough. It was no longer a strange cold place.
He had friends now, and friends led to friends,

and his health and physical vitality were assert-
ing themselves, driving him forward toward
what he had to have, and he had begun to learn
a little the ways of success, how it must be
watched and cosseted while it grew and grew,
fed by vitality. Already there were satellites,
people of lesser vitality who somehow fed off
him. And he had begun to understand the power
of his own good looks and physical charm. They
gave him an advantage; things, mostly little
things, for which others had to work seemed to
drop like ripe plums into his hands.

And then she began writing him from England. Once she wrote: "I am not an adventurer
like you. I don't expect things 'to turn up.'"
And he wrote back to her: "But things do 'turn
up,' just the same. They're beginning to turn up
for me. Maybe in another year I'll be making
plenty of money; maybe even in six months."

But even as he wrote he was aware that something inside him had changed and that inside
him there was no longer the ardor there had

once been. For a second he thought: "Perhaps she is right. Perhaps she should never come here at all. A foreigner, a Frenchwoman. It wouldn't be easy for her, or for me, either."

So long as he was free he could rise and rise, leaving behind him, to be forgotten, those who could not rise with him. Perhaps she herself could not accomplish it. There was no restlessness in her and no ambition. And then quickly the memory of the sandpit in the forest returned to him, making him physically ill with desire to recapture that wild sense of ecstatic annihilation and physical delight.

For days the memory returned to him again and again like a pain, mostly at night, so that he could not sleep for wanting her, and presently there arose in his mind the first seeds of cynicism. He found himself thinking: "Why should I suffer like this? Why should I not find it with some other girl? Why should I believe that she alone can give it me? It could not matter. She is the only one who will ever count.

She need never know. Even if she did know she would understand for she understands everything." And he began, slowly at first and shyly, the first of those pursuits which afterward became so common and promiscuous. The girl was an actress named Mary Carstairs, a small, neat little blonde who had come up from Georgia to make her way in the theater, and she was as bedazzled as himself by the city, and as eager to succeed. She did not ask him to marry her, for she, like himself, meant to be free. She fell in love with him, but he did not fall in love with her, and for a long time the thought of Eliane kept him from taking what was his to have for the taking. There was always the thought that some morning he would find a letter saying that she was on her way.

But the letter never came. Instead, he wakened one morning to find a letter from her saying that she had been married. She had married a distant cousin, she wrote, a fine man older than herself, a man who owned a great farm in

[146]

Normandy. She gave him no address, nor even told him her name. She wrote:

"It is better like this. You will think so, too, some day. We must be thankful for what we have had. Believe me, I have thought it over and over. I know how blessed we have been, and some day you will know, too. Now nothing can ever destroy what happened to us. I love you. I will love you always—the boy we found outside the gate by the side of the road.

"ELIANE."

He wrote to her, but there was never any answer; the letters were simply returned, worn and tattered and stamped, *"Addresse inconnue."* One phrase of the letter troubled him: "The boy we found outside the gate by the side of the road." Did she think he was different now? Did she know that he had changed? Did she suspect his doubts?

He went to Mary Carstairs, but that only lasted for a little time and he found nothing there of ecstasy or pain or delight, but only a diversion which brought him short periods of physical peace; and when he saw that Mary wanted more of himself than he was willing to give, he slipped away from her and the thing came to an end.

For a long time afterward he had no interest save for work, and that, he thought afterward, was perhaps very good for him. Perhaps Eliane had known that it would be good for him. And presently, because he was one of those born to success, the memory of the house and garden became something which belonged to the past and remained deep inside him, protected and hidden away. Successful people never know defeat or failure, not because they are of a different quality from others, but because for them there is no past, or even a present, but only the future.

Nevertheless, Eliane remained with him in a

strange way, especially in moments of weariness and discouragement, and when he fancied himself in love. She was always between him and every woman he ever knew, like a shadow, for she was the only woman he ever knew until Maisie who did not want something from him which he was unwilling to give. She was eternal. The others came and went, trivial, amusing, beautiful, plain, clever, and vain, but all of them egoists and wanting him for what they could get from him. They were always apart from him. And that game he knew better than any of them, and so none of it ever lasted.

Once, seven years after the Armistice, he went back to the house and garden in France, but it was empty and the shutters were up and the garden desolate. In the village they said that she had sold the house and gone away to England. The old gardener was dead and no one knew what had become of old Louise. It was market day, and as he walked through the streets of the village the country people gathered into little groups as the news spread that the "Américain" had returned. They stood in little clusters, like hens, looking after him and gossiping, so that he understood they had known the truth all along. Even the sleepy police commissioner had no idea what had become of her.

Part Three

Part Three

TWO WEEKS AFTER TOM LEFT THE HOSPITAL
they sailed, all of them—Sally, the two boys,
Nanny, and the dogs, on a slow boat to Havre,
Sally a little contemptuous because it was a
cheap boat and there was not a passenger aboard
whom she knew or had ever heard of. But there
was a crowd on the pier to see them off, made
up of successful and clever people, with flowers

[153]

and books and baskets of fruit and nuts, and that reconciled her a little because it made them all seem important in the eyes of the other passengers.

Jimmy Beaumont was there, in a checkered waistcoat, smoking his indestructible cigar. Tom noticed him growing more and more fidgety as the time for sailing drew near, and at last he said, "What's the matter with you this morning?" And Jimmy without a word drew him into a corner of the smoking-room. He could not at first bring himself to speak of the thing which obviously troubled him, but kept talking of trivialities until at last Tom said, "What's on your mind? Say it."

Jimmy shifted the cigar from one side of his mouth to the other and said: "It's about Maisie. Is that all finished?" It was the first time he had ever spoken of it thus, openly.

"Yes."

Jimmy looked at him sharply. "Are you sure?"

"What do you mean?"

"I mean is it over on both sides?"

"I think so. I gave her to understand that. I haven't written to her." But he felt the blood stealing into his face and for the first time in his life felt ashamed in front of Jimmy Beaumont.

"Okay," said Jimmy, and turned away, and as he turned Tom had a curious feeling that not only was he finished with Maisie, but with Jimmy Beaumont as well. There was something in the set of the manager's plump shoulders which was curiously final. And he wanted Jimmy to like him, to go on liking him.

Tom walked after him and said: "What d'you mean? Why do you ask me that?"

"Only on account of what I hear from the coast."

"What's that?"

"She's bitched everything. She had the biggest chance in the world."

"How?"

"She's been drinking. They can't get on with

[155]

the picture. She's costing them thousands because she's gone screwy—Maisie, who always behaves like a lamb when she's working." Tom looked away and Jimmy said, "She's acting as if she was ready to be shut up." He took the lapel of Tom's coat in his hand and said: "Listen, my boy. That's a great little actress. She means money and success to me and to you. Mebbe you'd better do something about it—not to mention what it means to her."

"I don't quite get you."

"Yes, you do, old fellow. Get one thing. When Jimmy Beaumont walks out on a woman it don't make any difference because all either of us ever wanted was a good time, but when you do it—especially to a woman like Maisie— it's a different story. You've got something I haven't got."

The bugle was blowing and there were shouts of, "All ashore." Weakly Tom said: "There isn't anything I can do now. It's too late."

But Jimmy turned away without answering

him and was gone down the gangplank, and in
a little while the boat was moving away from
the pier. Sally was standing beside him now,
waving and calling to the crowd on the pier,
which he saw only dimly because he was thinking of what he had lost—Maisie and Jimmy
Beaumont, the two people whom, with Nanny,
he trusted more than anyone on earth. But it *was*
too late, he kept telling himself. It was too late
if he meant to begin all over again with Sally
and keep his family together and find peace in
the house and garden by the river. There was
only one course to take, and that was to forget
Maisie, and now he knew that this was not
going to be so easy as it had seemed on the night
of the party. As Jimmy walked down the gangplank he had experienced a sudden moment of
clairvoyance in which he and Maisie were together again. Suddenly he remembered her letter: "We were meant for each other. We should
have come together long ago." Poor Maisie!

He and Sally had separate cabins. They saw

each other all day long, but at night they were
alone and he never went to her. It was a small
boat and a slow boat, and filled with people
who were either failures or had had no ambitions or were on their way to success, and at
first he found it hard to interest himself in them
—salesmen, spinsters on their way to cheap pen-
sions in Europe, comfortable middle-aged widows, a schoolmaster, all the people among
whom he had hoped to find peace. He knew
that he had no arrogance, but it was not easy to
fall back again into the habits of these people;
he had known only the clever ones for too long.
He tried to play, awkwardly, with the boys and
to interest them in the machinery of the old-
fashioned ship, but that, too, in another way,
was a failure. He had lost the habit, if he had
ever had it.

But Sally made no effort. She read book after
book and regarded her fellow passengers less
with contempt than with patient boredom. It
was an attitude which annoyed him, because

Sally in her own right had no reason for this arrogance. But for him she would have known only dull people, more glittery and trivial and silly than those solid members of society, but no more clever or intelligent. It was a pretentiousness of which he had been unaware before, because until now he had thought her merely superficial. And always, by hints, by overtures, by implications, she was saying to him, "Well, I hope you've got your fill of these people. You see what they're like."

It was not easy, this sudden dependence on each other, after so many years of speed and giddiness together and yet apart. In the evenings when the boys had gone to bed, he sometimes felt a sudden relief that he no longer had to play the rôle of father at which he found himself such a dub. But that strain was supplanted by another—the big strain of trying to make things go with Sally, who would not become any part of the life on the ship, but held aloof with a supercilious air of distaste. He was bored by

[159]

her. He had never known before how profoundly she bored him, because they had never
been alone, but always surrounded by people. If
only she had done things *with* him, and with
the other people on the ship, they would not
have been so dependent upon each other, and
so they would have escaped the tension created
by the sense of inadequacy. Dangerously he
found himself, in spite of everything, sometimes
thinking of Maisie, comparing her with Sally.
He told himself that he did this not because he
was in love with Maisie. He scarcely thought of
her at all in that way, but he could not escape
the certainty of how different the voyage would
have been with her in Sally's place. The ship
would not have been boring. The horseraces,
the dancing, the very conversation of the salesmen and widows, would have become ridiculous
and amusing and full of interest because of
some quality which Maisie brought with her.
Maisie was rowdy and human, and so she had
depths. But he could not bring himself to blame

Sally. It was not her fault that she was so different a kettle of fish, nor her fault that she had never known an existence, even with him, in which there was any human reality. He began to suspect that they should never have come away together, that the whole thing had been a mistake in the beginning, and that the whole struggle was of no use. He remembered that it was pity which had betrayed him, and he thought, "I must not feel sorry for Maisie and lose my head." He never thought, "Why should I not feel sorry for poor Maisie?"

Four days before the ship landed he began going to the bar after Sally had gone down to her cabin to lie between her own pink sheets to read until she fell asleep out of boredom, and in the bar he sat until it closed, drinking one whisky after another. It was the first time he had ever drunk like this. It made the voyage bearable.

He saw the little family into a hotel at St.

Brière. It was a small place. There was no casino nor were there fashionable restaurants and very few foreigners, and he thought, "Here we shall know peace," never thinking that the history of the dull voyage might only repeat itself. And as soon as they were settled he went off to Paris, and thence to the house and garden.

He hurried, as impatiently as if he were again a boy of twenty, absent on leave, crossing half of France to spend the night and say good-by to the girl with the dark hair and lips which curled at the corners. For the house and garden, as he drew nearer to it, had become an obsession. Without thinking of it, he had come to look upon them as a symbol of his salvation. They were an oasis in a desert. But it never occurred to him that he would not find what he had left so long ago, that the house and the garden would still be there, but that she would not be in them, moving about quietly, with her frank smile touched ever so lightly by the shadow of mockery. It did not occur to him that the peace of that enchanted world might only be desolation without her presence.

It was evening when he arrived, and he found the house empty. There had been tenants for a year or two from time to time, mostly painters who liked the study, but no one had cared enough for it to buy it, although it was for sale. With a fat, squat agent and a ring filled with heavy keys he went through the rooms again, dirty now, the furniture all covered with cotton sheets, and when he raised the sheets he found that the furniture was not the shabby ancient stuff which belonged to her, but suites of horrible stuff purchased wholesale from some Paris department store so that the house might be let. It was a strange house to him. The garden had changed less. Some one had made an ugly pair of circular flower beds in the lawn, but the little belvedere on the island was still there, and the ancient plane trees and the walled kitchen garden where he and Eliane had worked side by

[163]

side, only now it was empty and filled with
weeds.

The agent kept a running chatter, praising
the dreadful furniture and showing him all the
good points which did not interest him, because
an agent could not offer memories of which he
knew nothing; and at the end of the tour Tom
left the place in silence, feeling ill. And as he
locked the gate, out of the forest through the
still blue evening, across the marshes, came the
sound of a hunting-horn, and suddenly the enchantment returned and all at once he was not
standing in the dirty road outside the gate, but
was in the little belvedere on the island and
Eliane was there with him, saying, "It's the
huntsman's boy learning the calls. His father
was killed at Verdun last year."

Then he knew that he had to have this place,
and the old persistence and stubbornness which
had lain quiet in his spirit for so long were
roused. This was something he wanted, that he
could not do without, and he thought, "I will

[164]

bring it back to life again. I *will* have it back."
And for the first time in many months he felt
alive again.

The next day he bought the place, and before
he returned to St. Brière he engaged an architect and together they went over the house,
planning what must be done. Mostly it was an
affair of bathtubs and decoration and ridding
the house of the vile furniture. And now he
hated to leave it, for he was filled with a desire
to go to work at once to clean up the garden and
make it fertile again as it had been when Eliane
tended the plants with hands which were at
once strong and yet delicate.

When autumn came they found a school for
the boys, and Nanny went on a long holiday,
and Tom and Sally came alone to the house to
finish the decorating. It was a slow business,
and until there were rooms ready in which they
could live while the work progressed, they
stayed in a hotel two villages away. Tom chose

that instead of Paris because he knew that in
Paris the old life from which he wanted to
escape would begin all over again. There were
too many bars and there was the Ritz and the
Crillon. Sally was disappointed, but after a day
or two she forgot herself in the house.

When first he took Sally to see the place she
was silent when he showed her about, and he
felt bitterly toward her when her only comment
was that the situation was low, and that archi-
tecturally the place had not much to offer, and
that certainly it would be damp. All her life
she had been used to houses already decorated,
heated, and luxurious, into which she moved
with the least possible trouble.

"It's a whim," she said, "which is going to
cost you a lot of money."

"Why a whim?" he asked.

"Because you'll get tired of it and want something else. It's always been like that."

He did not answer her, but he understood
that of course she saw it as something quite dif-

ferent from himself. To her it was simply a nondescript house set down in the midst of a ragged garden by the edge of a swamp.

But once they set to work she became interested, in a way he had never thought possible, and presently they lost themselves completely in bringing life once more to the house. No longer were they two people, apart, separate, striving to understand each other. It was the happiest time they had ever known together, happier even than a honeymoon when they had begun almost at once to have misgivings.

In old clothes they worked together in the garden, watching the workmen, talking with the architect, planting shrubs and plants, and two days a week they went to Paris to buy furniture and chintzes and dishes, and one day a week they climbed into the motor and went from village to village, exploring the countryside and visiting shops where antiques were sold. They were never bored with each other, because all day long they were active, and in the evenings

[167]

when dinner was finished, they separated and went to bed. Sally was happy because she was busy and because she was spending money. Buying things always gave her pleasure.

Alone in bed at night, Tom sometimes lay awake thinking about the house and their lives and sometimes of Maisie and sometimes of Eliane and sometimes of Malcolm James. He knew that sometimes Sally had letters from Malcolm, but she never spoke of them or talked of him, and only once did she speak of Maisie, and that was when they talked of his new play and she said, "Will Maisie be in it?"

"I don't know," he answered, lying.

"You'll have to be going back for it soon."

"I'm not going back for it," he said.

"But you'll have to."

He frowned and was silent for a time. And then he tried to explain to her that he had meant all along just what he said when he told her the plan of escaping for good. "I'm not going to do any of the things which one has to do to be successful. I've been doing that all my life. That's what's the matter with me and I'm finished."

"I think you're being a fool," she said. "What can you, of all people, do without plenty of money?"

"I did without it once. I was a damned sight better off."

But she only laughed and said, "All right. Suit yourself. But I hope you won't mind if I take a trip away now and then to relieve the monotony."

He knew perfectly well that Maisie was not going to be in the play, for Beaumont had written she was not. He couldn't, he wrote, take the risk of opening with her and having her out of the cast a week later. It was bad enough having to open without Tom being there. Maisie, he wrote, had taken to drinking steadily. Sometimes she was no good at all for weeks at a time. And in one letter he asked: "Why don't you write to her? A word or two from you might buck her up."

But Tom didn't answer the question at all. It was none of Beaumont's business, and he had no right to blame him because Maisie chose to get drunk. He tried not to think of her, but the memory of her would come over him again and again at moments when he least expected it. When he was bored or irritated with Sally, he would think what fun it would be if Maisie were there instead of Sally, working with him. Sally kept destroying the feeling of permanence which he was forever trying to build up about the adventure. She treated the whole thing as a lark which would come to an end presently, and when she went in to Paris alone, he knew that she went at once to the Ritz and that she had seen friends and acquaintances out of that giddy world he had left behind. She never spoke of them and none of them ever appeared, but for a day or two after each trip she would be bored and restless. Outwardly she was doing her best to make the thing go, but inwardly all her spirit was fighting him. She was fighting the house, the escape, even the idea of reconciliation. She had no desire for roots. She wanted, he knew, to drift as she had always done. And she was determined to win or smash everything. Her weapons were invisible ones.

They had one quarrel, and that came when the over-expensive bar, all complete, arrived from Paris and was set up before he discovered it, in the old study of Monsieur Vainville.

For a long time now he had been aware that instead of recapturing the spirit of the house, it eluded him more and more, escaping farther and farther into the distance with each new piece of furniture and bit of chintz. Slowly it became a charming and even beautiful house, but it was not the same. It had nothing to do with the charm and comfort of that room in which he had awakened one late afternoon seventeen years before, or that kitchen in which he and Eliane had cooked their suppers with the fire shining on the copper kettles. Each day, it seemed, they destroyed more of that feeling of peace and stillness. He never spoke of it to Sally, for she would never have understood; but the knowledge baffled and irritated him. He saw presently that it was not the house which he had wanted above all else in the world; it was the sense of still eternity which he had found in the presence of Eliane, that feeling of calm and certainty he had never known save when he had lived here with her. And each day between them he and Sally drove her presence farther and farther from the house. It was almost as if Sally *knew* and set out to defeat him with her expensive antiques, her mirrored bathrooms, her bar on wheels.

The morning the bar appeared he knew suddenly what lay at the root of their failure; they had made a house not for peace and solitude, where they might live quietly in happiness. They had made a house for parties and people, a lovely house, but one which needed to be

[172]

filled with noise and confusion. He did not know which of them was to blame, although he suspected that Sally had done her part knowingly, and the sight of the bar made him feel that she had been cheating all along and put him into a fury.

He accused her of having double-crossed him and told her to send back the bar, and then she, too, lost her temper.

"Either the bar stays or I go," she said.

"I won't have my house made into a roadhouse for all the bums in creation."

"So all my friends are bums! They're your friends, too!"

There was an element of terror in the violence of the quarrel, as if suddenly they were stripped naked of all pretenses, of all consideration for each other, of all dreaming. They stood there facing each other in the study of old Monsieur Vainville, across the shining new bar, all his disillusionment and boredom showing in his face, all her hatred of him for his egotism and

[173]

aloofness. And then all at once he collapsed, more out of weariness than for any other reason.

"Don't let's do this," he said. "Don't! For God's sake, don't! Let's never see each other again, but let's not be beasts."

And she began to cry, and in a little while there was peace again, after a fashion, but in his heart there rose the terror that the whole thing was destined to collapse in failure.

The house was finished a little before Christmas, and when the boys came home from school there were two rooms ready for them and a room for Nanny. The boys were pleased and spent their first day exploring the stables and punting about the pond the leaky old boat. Tom thought, "We'll have an old-fashioned Christmas. It's fun to be together once more."

Sally seemed contented, and together they went shopping for Christmas gifts in Paris. In the back of his mind lay the memory of Christmas in Aunt Cassie's house, the table laden with food, the tree ornamented with tin foil and strings of popcorn and gifts for everyone which had cost nothing at all because no one ever had any money. It was something which had disappeared, but in spite of everything he meant to recapture the spirit, here in another country, in a strange house. And so to recapture it fully he tried to buy it, spending extravagant sums and going to all the expensive shops. But when Christmas morning came the spirit had escaped him. They gathered round a tree hung with decorations of crystal and silver, and opened package after package—jewelry and perfume and furs for Sally, an electric train, motor-boats, and German kodaks for the boys, wonderful things for himself, but in all the boxes there was not so much Christmas spirit as he had found long ago when he unwrapped a bit of paper saved from the box in which Aunt Cassie's new hats had come from Montgomery Ward and found inside a dollar watch.

The house was new and they were strangers

in it. For none of them but himself was there any association of any kind. There were no roots, and not even the feeling of a house which had been loved and lived in by others for generation after generation; somehow he and Sally had destroyed even that. And outside there was no snow nor any sound of sleigh-bells, but only dampness and darkness which fell a little after three o'clock, when a slow fog rose off the marshes.

That night the boys went to bed late, and for a time he and Sally sat before the fire, trying to pretend it had been a good Christmas, but in their hearts they were uneasy and bored. Sally, he knew, because she was restless, and himself because, in spite of everything, he had failed. When she went to bed at last he took a letter from his pocket and tore it open. He had had it there all day, since early morning, without daring to open it, and now when he was alone he poured himself a double whisky and sat down to read it. It was short. It read:

"DEAR TOM: I hope this will reach you as near as possible on Xmas day. It's just a line to let you know that I'm thinking of you and will be thinking of you on Xmas. Perhaps I shouldn't have written at all, but I think you'll forgive me. It isn't much and it makes me happy to think that even if you never read it, you'll at least hold it in your hands for a moment before throwing it into the fire. That will be a small bond between us—the smallest, but something. Jimmy gave me your address. I've been ill. That's why I couldn't do your play. But it's a success, so I don't suppose it matters much. I'm better now. I've got a job in a good play. We open after New Year's. Merry Christmas, Tom. I love you always.

"MAISIE."

When he had finished, he tore it up and threw it into the fire and took another drink. A little after three o'clock he went to bed, drunk.

The drinking, in moments when he was alone and thoughtful, astonished him—that it was so easy to escape by simply drinking a bottle of whisky. He drank only in moments of complete weariness and despair, when his nerves became over-sensitive and irritable and the slightest incident was enough to throw him into melancholia or a wild rage. In more normal moments he came to regard himself with detachment, from a distance, as another person, and in the end contemplation of the spectacle served only to aggravate his unhappiness. He knew that he was a pest and a trial to Sally, and that he ought not to blame her if in her efforts to make things go well between them she blundered and annoyed and bored him. She was, he knew, a kind of hothouse plant who had grown up sheltered and protected from every frost of disappointment and every blast of disillusionment. She had none of that *awareness* which is so much the equipment of every adventurer in life; she could neither divine a situation by means of an extra sense nor fathom the reasons why a husband who was rich and successful and had everything in life should be such a brooding bore. But he knew, too, that if he did not him-self know what the trouble was, he could not expect her to find it.

He was aware only that there was something missing from his life, something profound and fundamental. At moments he believed that it was love, but in his heart he knew that it was not love he wanted, unless it was the love he had experienced long ago with Eliane, and that could never come to him again, scarred as he was with the wounds of so many adventures and so much experience.

And when he tried to work, nothing came of it, either of his efforts to write a play which got beneath the surface of life, or to concoct those successful entertainments which once he had found so easy to do. A chill paralysis took possession of his intellect and his emotions, and when the sense of his own futility took possession of him he would begin drinking again. The presence of Sally in the same house only bored and irritated him, as much, he knew, as he bored and irritated her. Every evening after the darkness and mist came down they would sit in the same room before the fire, surrounded by silence and glass and chintz and books and comfort, by all the things which they had bought together to ease his restlessness and misery, but the room might as well have been an empty barn, for all the warmth and intimacy there was in it.

And then one day in March when the days were growing longer, Sally came to him and said: "Tom, I can't stand it any longer. I've got to have a holiday. I want to go to America for three or four weeks."

At first he was glad with that sudden sure

pleasure which springs from the instinct, untainted by thought or reflection.

He said, "Yes, I think it would be a good thing to do. You've been very sporting."

"It isn't that," she said, "but I'm afraid if I don't have a change I'll fail altogether."

So they planned when she would leave, and presently she went upstairs, and when she came down she carried a half-dozen letters in her hands.

"It's about the boys," she said. "They hate it in England."

"They never told me so."

"No. They only write it to me. They told me at Christmas."

"Why didn't they tell me?"

She was silent for a moment, as if not wanting to tell him, and then she said: "They're afraid of you, Tom. Young Tom said he felt he didn't know you well enough to discuss it."

For a moment he suspected her morbidly of plotting in devious ways, unscrupulously as she had sometimes done in the past, to get what she wanted by any means possible; but the letters killed the suspicion. They were short and the two written by young Tom were filled with misspellings. They wanted to go back to America. They hated the school and the damp Oxfordshire village. They were homesick, not, it seemed, for either himself or Sally or even the house, but for America and the dry, crisp snow of winter and the rocky landscape of Connecticut. The letters touched him because of their spirit. The two boys were doing their best to make it a go, but one got out of the childish scrawls a feeling that they had been uprooted and were withering in a strange country. Young Tom wrote, "Don't tell Daddy."

For a long time he sat in silence, staring into the fire, and at last he said: "I suppose they should go home. You can take them back with you."

"Yes, that's what I thought."

"We'll look up boats."

"What will you do?" asked Sally.

"I'll stay here. I've got to make it a go. They can come back for the summer."

He saw that she was pleased, and for a moment he was angry because in her smiling eyes was the implication that she had been right from the beginning, but he only said, "Could I keep the letters?"

"If you like."

He took them with him to his room and locked them in a drawer. They made him feel incredibly lonely, but when he thought of it he saw that it was he who had created his own loneliness. He had been ruthless once more, as he had always been, not through egotism or even through selfishness, but through something else. He had torn the two boys from their roots and tried to plant them elsewhere, without even talking to them of it. They were afraid of him. They didn't know him well enough.

Sally left at the end of the month, and when

[183]

he saw her and the boys aboard the ship at Southampton he felt a sudden pang and a softening that went all through him, not so much because Sally was leaving as for all the associations of their life together. He had a feeling that she would not return and that everything was finished. But it was better this way. There were no scenes, no quarrels, no emotional goings-on, but he had a dim sense of having failed at living.

He had hoped, half believing it, that when he was alone in the house everything would change and that he would begin to write again and find at least the satisfaction of turning out good journeymen's work. But when he came back to the empty house he found it a chill and unfamiliar place. The presence of Eliane and the solid peace which came to him even in the memory of her were no longer there. They had been driven out by the expensive chintzes and furniture and the bar. It was a house made for parties, not good to stay in alone.

His work went no better, and in the evenings

boredom descended upon him, a different sort of boredom from that he knew when Sally sat opposite him, remote and restless, but a boredom just as bad. Sometimes in the evenings when he sat in the little belvedere far from the house, listening to the huntsmen practicing in the twilight, the presence of Eliane returned for a little time.

There came a time when he could bear it no longer and he went to Paris straight to the Ritz, and there he found again that world of glittering people which he had abandoned, years ago it seemed to him, although it had been only for a little time. They were all there, the writers, the millionaires, the divorcees, the kept women, the actors. In that world even gigolos were successful. There he found all the old glitter and excitement, all the sense of haste and recklessness. By three in the afternoon he was quite drunk, from drinking to celebrate his return to the world of worldliness. It went, the celebration, from bar to bar, from restaurant to restaurant, from night club to night club, faster and faster, until a little before dawn the false gaiety began to seep out of him, leaving him cold and miserable and abysmally drunk, wondering what it was he sought that the others seemed to have kept and he had lost. The others, he thought dully, looking round the room, were all failures at the business of living—all these people who were so successful.

And most of them asked him for news of Maisie, but he had none. He put them off by saying that he heard from time to time and that there was no news, but among them there were two who had seen her. She was ill, they said, and one of them added, what Jimmy had told him, that she had been drinking and that it was impossible for her to work any more.

He wakened at five the next day in his hotel, and lay for a time listening to the noises in the street outside, feeling soiled and miserable, and when he rose he had a drink, and then, feeling better, dressed and went out. And so the old life began all over again, only worse than before, because now he had no direction and no plan, and whatever he did was by chance and without motive, and wherever he went there was no reason for it.

Bitterly he thought: "That damned house was made for parties. I'll satisfy it. I'll give it all the parties it wants, God damn it!"

And so he asked people to the old gray house, anyone, sometimes friends, but more and more often people he met in bars whom he scarcely knew at all, people now who weren't even successful and clever, but hangers-on and parasites. They came in expensive motors and drank huge quantities of gin and whisky. Servants left because of the disorderly life, but new ones came to replace them for three or four days until they too, shocked, gave notice and fled.

It had never been like this with him before. In the old days he had always kept life in control; there were even times when, as a spectator, he had watched the others without himself taking part. And he had never had the same sort of people to his house. Now, day by day, the whole group degenerated. He had casual squalid love-affairs with women for whom he had nothing but contempt. It was as if, since the spirit of the house had eluded him, he was determined to have his revenge on it by thrusting it deeper and deeper into confusion and noise and mud. It was as if he sought to revenge himself upon himself for being what he was, and he was aware, too, at times of a strange sense of purification, as if he would purge himself by debauchery until through satiation and disgust he would emerge clean and fresh and ready to begin life over again. He no longer read nor wrote anything at all, and when letters came from Sally or from the boys they sometimes lay for days about the house without being opened. When he did read them they conveyed little impression beyond the fact that they were all happier now in America, "Because they are away from me," he thought, bitterly.

The study of old Monsieur Vainville was always filled with people now, and the bar worked overtime—the bar which Sally had installed, perhaps because she knew him better than he knew himself.

At the end of May a letter came from Sally. He knew the handwriting well enough, but the house was full of people and his head wasn't clear and so he tossed it aside into a drawer to wait until he was alone again, and for three days he did not know that what he suspected that rainy day at Southampton was true. She was never coming back, and after thirteen years their life together had come to an end. She wrote quite simply:

"I've tried to face it, my dear, but I can't and there's no use in our going on making each other miserable. I can't even say 'for the sake of the children'—because they'll really be hap-

pier and better off visiting us sepa-
rately than living in an atmosphere
which is dead and full of boredom
and sometimes of worse. It would
never be any better—worse, if anything—because sooner or later we'd
begin to quarrel and hate each other,
and that we shouldn't do on the boys'
account. There's no use in staying together, trying to make go what won't
go. It'll do no one any good and certainly will do all of us harm. My
mother and father were like that. They
went on respectably living together,
hating each other and when my father
died I was glad, because it meant that
I would have a little peace. I think in
the end they came to enjoy their hatred
of each other, but they never thought
of me. Children are clever that way
and they know so much more than we

[190]

think. It's only right that the boys should spend half their time with you, if you want them.

"I want to marry Malcolm James.

"I know what you think. You're saying, 'How can she leave me for a dull idiot like that' (and at the same time thinking, 'Thank God she's leaving me'). 'What can she see in him, middle-aged and beefy, going to the office at nine and coming home, after stopping at the club, at seven.' Yes, I know it's all true. So what!

"I'll tell you what, my dear. Malcolm is what I've been looking for all my life. He's not so good looking as you. He isn't one-tenth as clever or intelligent. You have fifteen times as much charm (too damned much). You're fifty times as popular (too damned popular). But it doesn't make

any difference. It's Malcolm I want
and Malcolm I've been looking for
always.

"I thought I'd found him in you
long ago that night in the bar in
Cannes when I cried and you talked
so much good sense to me and then
asked me to marry you. I didn't know
then how damned clever you were and
that you could talk good sense and
give a perfect impersonation of Malcolm James (which means peace and
solidity and comfort) and never mean
a word of it. I found it out only after
we were married, and then I discovered you weren't a sturdy oak at all,
but only some kind of seaweed, slipping and slithering away (with great
charm), never facing anything and
making the clinging vine try to stand
up of its own strength. You see, Tom,
I've never been able to put my finger

on you for one minute in all the years we've been married.

"I never liked the life we had very much, but I've never known any other kind. I didn't know how to lead any other kind of life. I wanted somebody to show me. You must have known a solid life as a boy, but you never told me anything about it. You see, Malcolm is dumb and dull, but he's a rock and I'm so tired I want a rock to cling to.

"I don't know when you got this obsession about that house you're living in, but knowing you, I suspect there was a woman mixed up in it, otherwise you wouldn't have seen a perfectly plain house and garden as paradise. I was willing to make a try of it, but I knew from the beginning it wasn't any good, because you really don't want all that peace and quiet you

[193]

talked about. Maybe you've found it, now that I've cleared out. Certainly I was no help and I know it, and I know you were blaming me all the time because you couldn't find what you'd expected to find. I suspect that's something that comes from the inside out and not the outside in. And there's no use running away from one country to another. You always have to take yourself along.

"Knowing you, I'd say that you have something on your mind. It isn't Maisie, by any chance, is it? I hear she's going to the dogs as fast as she can. You were probably too nice and charming to her and she fell in love with you. I'll confess now that I never did. You'll say to yourself that I'm too shallow ever to know what love is and perhaps that's true. Well, I shouldn't mind Maisie as a successor, except per-

[194]

haps as an influence (together with your own selfishness) on the boys. But we're getting on, Tom. Thirty-eight isn't first youth any longer. It's time to begin thinking about settling down."

The rest of the letter was all about lawyers and arrangements, amazingly business-like, he thought, for Sally, and at the end she wrote:

"I'm still fond of you, Tom, even when you're a brute, but it's better for everybody that we stop pretending. You are a brute, you know, only such a subtle one that nobody could ever prove it. I hope we'll go on being friendly and see each other now and then. I'd even ask you to come and visit us when we're married, but I know Malcolm wouldn't like it. He's too old-fashioned."

He had known all along that it was coming,

but the cold fact shocked him now, leaving him with a faint feeling of sickness. And the letter made him see Sally in a new way, more intelligent and desirable than he had ever imagined her to be. She knew, he now saw, so much more than he had ever imagined she knew, and he wondered why she had never spoken until now; perhaps, he thought, because words being my business, I am so much better at using them than she is, and so she never dared to say any of those things. Or maybe she never understood what was lacking in their marriage until she experienced this ripe love for Malcolm James and the security he offered. At any rate, she had used words damned well in her letter. But then it only proved what he always knew, that anyone could use words if the emotion behind them was strong enough.

It was ten o'clock in the morning when he read the letter, and he began to drink almost at once, to destroy the feeling of depression with which it left him. And at two o'clock he packed a suitcase, told the servants he was going away indefinitely, and went off to Paris. There he drank some more, but the depression didn't leave him. He kept worrying over the letter, even in the midst of drinking with friends. And he kept thinking: "It's all a gamble and somebody has to lose. If she'd found Malcolm James and I'd married Eliane, everything would have been different." Married to the still peace of Eliane he wouldn't be sitting now in a bar, miserable and unhappy, because a wife whom he wanted to leave him *was* leaving him.

And through the haze of alcohol the old obsession of Eliane returned to him and he felt a fierce desire to return again to his youth and to that damned house he had ruined and defiled. At any rate, he had to be alone, away from all these noisy, trivial, and silly people, and so, suddenly without excusing himself, he rose and left the bar, climbed into the car without even troubling to pick up the suitcase at the hotel.

"I'm drunk," he thought. "All I want is to be

back there in the house, alone." And then as he pulled himself together to steer the car through the streets of Paris into the open country, something occurred to him which he had never thought of before. Perhaps all those people he had just left behind him, all those Americans, all those cheap, clever men and idle women, were as miserable as himself. Perhaps there was something profoundly wrong in their background, in their upbringing, something at the very root of all their lives.

By the time he reached the gateway where he had fallen off the motorcycle long ago, he was sobered a little, enough for him to get down and open the gate himself, aware that he did not want the new servants to see him, not because he was drunk, but because he hated the idea of all servants and especially strange ones. He drove the car across the courtyard and into the garage made from the cow stable where once he had milked cows each morning and evening. He saw no one, and the idea suddenly came to him that the servants had taken advantage of his absence to go away, leaving the house empty, and he was filled with a sudden blind fury at their disloyalty; and then almost at once he thought, "Why should they be loyal to a fellow like me?"

But as he passed the gate into the vegetable-garden he caught sight of a woman's figure on the path under the ancient fruit trees. He would not have troubled to discover who it was and would have gone directly into the house, save that there was something dimly familiar about it. Stopping, he stood looking down the path, and then slowly he saw what he could not believe.

It was the way she moved which caught his attention, for he had never seen but one woman in the world who walked thus, lightly yet firmly, as if she drew strength from the earth with each step. And then for a moment he was terrified, thinking either that he was mad or that he saw a ghost.

[199]

The figure was heavier and dressed all in black, with a flowing veil of crêpe. She carried an umbrella and a bag of heavy black leather such as the wives of rich farmers carry. There was nothing smart about the woman; rather she looked provincial and dowdy.

Steadying his shaking nerves, he went through the gateway and along the path, his heart pounding against his waistcoat. She did not turn until he was nearly upon her and she, startled, heard the sound of gravel crunching beneath his feet. When she did turn, they stood looking at each other for a moment without speaking.

Then all he said was, "Eliane!"

"Tom!"

He did not kiss her lips, for it would have been like kissing the lips of a ghost, and besides there were all those years between them, making strangers of them, but he took both her hands, and then, after another silence, he said, "How did you come here?"

Her answer broke down the barrier of the

years. She chuckled, and the old look of mischief, a little ripened, a little more knowing, came into her eyes.

"I'm a trespasser," she said. "I broke in. You can have me arrested by French law. You can even shoot me and get off."

She said it in English and he saw at once that she had almost lost the knack of speaking it. The accent was heavier and the words came with difficulty, so that he began to laugh. She laughed, too, and laughing, they walked up the garden path toward the house. His arm slipped about her waist, plumper now than it had once been, but, oddly enough, after so many years and so much experience—shyness returned to him, the old shyness he had felt in the same garden so long ago.

What he had suspected was true. The servants were all gone; they must have gone to Paris for a holiday soon after his car disappeared down the road. He should have been angry at their leaving the house unwatched, but nothing mattered now; and he was even glad because there was no one there to disturb the peace and the sense of delight which she seemed to have brought back with her to the house.

All the doors were locked and all the shutters barred, so that he had to smash a window of the study to get in. Once inside, she made tea for them and she told him how she came to be there.

She had come up to Paris from Normandy to buy clothes and seeds and gramophone records, and when all her tasks were finished she felt an overpowering desire to revisit the house which she had not seen since it was sold, fifteen years before. She did not know to whom it belonged nor who was living in it, but on the chance that it was some one friendly who would let her in the gate, she took the train and walked over from the village. At the gate she rang the bell again and again, but no one answered and so she thought, for all the new paint on the gate, that the place must be empty.

"It was very simple," she said. "I walked around through the forest and came in by the river side across the bridge." She thrust out her provincial boots. "Look," she said. "I'm covered with mud. I held up my skirts and walked through the shallow pond. I had to see it again, after I came all this way. I simply had to see it."

"And now you're going to stay for a time?"

But she only laughed again and said, "No, I have to go back by the train that leaves at five fifty-seven. I have to be in Rouen early tomorrow morning."

"Why?" he asked.

"Because it's the spring cattle-market."

"And what has that to do with you?"

"Because I'm a farmer now. It's business. I've got some of the finest beef cattle in all of France."

There was pride in her voice, and when she told him about the cattle a light came into her eyes, and, watching her, he was troubled and almost resentful that she should seem so strong and so contented and that the years had treated her so lightly. It would have been right if she had been as miserable and as unhappy as himself. That was the way it would have been in a book.

"And you ought to see my Percherons," she said. "The finest horses in all France."

Listening and planning, he asked, "When does your train leave Paris for Rouen?"

"Ten fifteen."

He thought quickly and then said, "Stay and we'll cook supper the way we used to do, and I'll drive you in to Paris in time to catch the train."

The idea pleased her and she agreed, and when they had finished tea she said, "Take me all over the house now. I want to see everything."

And so he took her from room to room, showing her the baths and the expensive chintzes and the fine rugs, and all the while she chattered and felt the stuffs and admired all the modern bits. Last of all they came to the room where he had wakened to see the forest and marshes through the window for the first time, and the cat was asleep on the window sill. It was his room now, done brightly in gay colors, and when they entered it she fell silent and did not speak until they left it. He knew then that she was feeling what he felt, and that she, too, experienced a shadow of the wild delight they had known together in this room so long ago. For a moment he thought: "Perhaps we could bring it back now. Perhaps we could recapture a little of it." But he looked at her sharply and divined almost at once that it could not be. There were too many years between and too much experience and too much knowledge. For that they would have to be young again, each of them finding love for the first time. Until this moment he had thought that nothing was changed, save that they were older, but now suddenly he knew that in a way they had become strangers. They did

not know each other at all. They did not know
what had happened to each other in all that
time. On his side there were the shadows of
women, some loved and many unloved, between
them spoiling all the freshness of what had happened long ago.

When they left the room she said: "It's your
house now. It isn't mine any more."

"What d'you mean?"

"I mean it's exactly like you."

"The way I am now?"

"No, the way you were even then, bright and
gay and full of excitement. When I lived here
it was slow and old and a little shabby."

They found eggs in the kitchen and salad in
the garden and Tom drove into the village for
a steak, and when he came back he found her
already at work, dressed in an overall of the
cook. She was fascinated by the modern stove
and the box which made ice by electricity and
the pots and pans made not of copper, but of
aluminum. The great coal range of her day was

gone and its fire no longer reflected itself in the copper kettles hung against the wall.

"Your cook," she said, "is a dirty woman. Look!" And she opened the door of a cupboard and showed him the dust that lay on the shelves. "You need looking after. They're probably swindling you. Anyway, you'll have to send them all away after today."

"Why don't you stay and look after me?"

But she only laughed and said, "No. I've got cattle and horses and a thousand acres of land and three sons."

"Three! I've got only two sons."

"Well, you see," she said, laughing at him, "I'm still the stronger. Go and fetch the wine and I'll tell you about them."

When he returned with a bottle of Burgundy the supper was laid out, the salad crisp and green, the steak thick and done exactly right, lying in a nest of crisp fried potatoes and cress which had come from the clean swift-flowing little river. He remembered suddenly that this was the first real meal he had had in months which had not begun with a half dozen cocktails.

"Now tell me," he said.

Suddenly she became grave and told the story. When he went away, she thought at first that she was going to die, except that all her family had strong constitutions and none of them had ever died of love, no matter how hard they tried.

"But just the same," she said, "I lost weight and grew pale and my father was worried. He knew what was the matter and he knew how cruel it was—that I should have for a lover a stranger, a foreigner who had to go back to his own country. And then he died, and that helped a little because it took my mind off you. And when he was dead I went to England where I'd been very happy as a girl, and stayed there with some friends of mine. They were very kind to me, the way the English are."

At the beginning of the next winter she returned to France and went to stay with cousins in Normandy, and that was the way she met her husband. He was a distant cousin, a man fifteen years older than herself who was a widower with no children.

"I liked the life," she said, simply, "and when he asked me to marry him I accepted. He was a good man—a big, tall, blond man like yourself, only older and more solid and calm. I came to love him very much." Her face grew more serious. "He died a year ago. He went out one night during a storm to open the gates in the water meadows and came back wet to the waist. He died of pneumonia and so I have to run the farm until the boys grow up. The oldest is only twelve."

He tried to say something which would express a sympathy which he should have felt and did not, but he could not find words. The dead man he had never seen, and there was all this between him and Eliane which made the man seem an outsider. He mumbled a few words and then said, "Were you still in love with me when you married him?"

"Yes," she said, smiling. "I was in love with you and I still am in love with you, not with what you are now—sitting there opposite me, looking very ill and a little drunk, but what you were then. You see what happened to us was very rare. It hardly ever happens to anyone, and we didn't spoil it and so it's mine forever. Even now I can think about it and be happy. I suppose I'll be thinking about it when I'm an old woman. We're both changed and this house isn't the same any more, but it's still alive for me. The old house exists and it always will so long as I'm alive." She looked away from him, "And the sandpit and the forest. Nothing can ever destroy them for me."

"Then why did you marry him instead of me?"

For a moment she was silent, and then she smiled and said: "Because things have to go on. That's quite another story. I doubt if you'd understand. You're American and very young."

"Tell me," he said.

"It takes a long time and it might bore you."

"No, tell me. It might help a little. There's still a sore place where you hurt me."

"It was better like that—to hurt you, just to disappear and have it end like that, with no quarrels or letters or seeing each other again." She rose to bring the coffee, and when she sat down and filled his cup and hers, she went on:

"Supposing I had waited and married you, what would have happened? You wouldn't have come here to live in France. That would have been your death. You had everything to do, all your life and career to make, and you couldn't make it in a foreign country which you didn't understand. So I should have had to come to you. I'd have waited until you made enough money and then I'd have come to you and everything would have been wrong, because I belong here as much as you belong there. You couldn't have transplanted me, because my roots go very deep, and when you tried to move me the roots would wither. I'd have been miserable and I would have made you miserable, and presently we'd have quarreled and separated, and we would have wasted years and have spoiled the wonderful thing that happened to us. That would have been too bad."

She stopped talking for a moment, but he said nothing, and presently she continued:

"It wasn't altogether that, either. It all goes much deeper. I know it's hard for you to see, because you're a romantic. You're still one, or you wouldn't have come back to this house and you wouldn't be a little drunk right now. Well, so am I, but in a different way. I'm romantic about carrying on life and traditions and things like that. Love is wonderful, but it isn't everything, and in spite of what people say it doesn't go on forever. Love goes and people stay together because they are friends and are used to each other and like the same things, but to stay together you have to have roots and grow into life itself." She smiled and touched his hand. "You haven't any roots, dear Tom. You never had any. I knew it long ago. You've got ambition and restlessness and a passion for success, but you haven't any roots. You never had any, and to build families and traditions and inheritances and a life that goes on and on, you have to have roots and be attached to things.

"When you used to tell me about what you meant to do in life, it made me feel sick, because I knew that whenever you talked like that you were an adventurer at heart and that nothing could ever come of what began here. D'you remember that on the night you were hurt you picked yourself up and bandaged your own head and got back on the motorcycle and set off again because you *had* to be in St. Quentin by daylight? You've been getting to St. Quentin by daylight ever since. You always will be, even when you're an old man. And I'm content to

[213]

stay where I am. What happened with us here in this house was an accident of Nature. It wasn't meant to go on. Nature didn't care anything about that."

She laughed suddenly. "Maybe I shouldn't say this. Maybe I'll hurt you because you're a romantic. I'm only a farmer and a cattle-breeder and a Frenchwoman. But this is what you never saw and never will see. Nature made us like that, to fall in love and sleep together just to have children and carry on. She isn't interested in romance and sentiment and sentimentality. That's what we build up around ourselves when we fall in love. We try to make falling in love go on and on because it's such pleasant agony, but Nature doesn't care anything about that. When she has accomplished what she wanted she doesn't care any more what happens to poor things like us who have done what she meant us to do. And that's the way it is. You see, I didn't want to be outwitted by Nature. And I was thinking of you too, my dear. It wouldn't have been any better for you, although it would have been easier because you haven't any roots."

She looked at her watch and rose and began clearing away the dishes. He helped her as he had done long ago, and she said: "But you haven't told me what happened to you. I know you're successful. I see your name sometimes in the London *Times*. But then I always knew you would be. Nothing could have stopped you but death."

And he began to tell her his story, shyly at first and then with a sense of shame, for as he talked he began to see that what he had to tell sounded peculiarly close to a record of failure. Even when he told her of the fame he had and the money he had made, the story sounded empty and hollow, and when he came to the part about Sally and the children he found himself changing facts and trying to make the story sound less barren and awful.

But she was not deceived. Her face grew still

and grave as she listened, and at last she said, "And so now you've gone to pieces?"

"Yes."

"It won't last unless you let it."

He did not answer her, and she said, suddenly, "You've been drinking too much for a long time."

"Yes."

"And other things."

"Yes."

"You mustn't pity yourself."

"No, I try not to do that. I never did until lately."

"It never does any good." She kept on drying the dishes. "There's only one thing to do."

"What?"

"Get out of this house and never come back to it."

"It cost me a lot of money."

"What difference does that make if it destroys you?"

"I can't go back to America."

"Why not?"

Again he was silent. She put the plates into the cupboard and then said, "Is there something on your conscience?"

"Yes."

He did not want to tell her about Maisie. She waited for a moment and then said: "All right. Don't tell me. I know what you ought to do."

"What?"

"Come to Normandy to visit me."

The idea startled him at first, and then it seemed a solution, the only possible one. He could not imagine coming back alone to the house, for in the last hour he had come to hate it more than ever, and he could not go back to Paris and the life he had been leading.

"But I don't even know your name," he said.

She smiled. "Madame Pierre Harcourt—known in the countryside as the widow Harcourt—a woman who can look out for herself and drive a sharp bargain."

"I'll come," he said. "I'll drive you there to-

night. Have you anything in Paris? It's nearer
to go direct from here by way of Beauvais."

"I travel light. It's all in my bag."

And so they drove hour after hour and arrived in the dark streets of Rouen at midnight
and from then on Eliane showed him the way.
The farm lay an hour and a half farther on, and
on the way, a little after they had turned off the
highroad into a deep lane bordered by great
beech trees, they came suddenly round a curve
into the midst of a herd of cattle. The beasts,
dazzled by the headlights, scattered in all directions, and when Tom had stopped the car Eliane
got down and began driving them all to one
side of the road. Two drovers in smocks appeared, and behind them a dozen or more giant
Percherons, two stallions and the rest mares,
tied together in lots of four. Eliane began shout-
ing at the drovers, giving directions and calling
them by name, "Pierre!" and "Jean!" and
"Etienne!" and in a little while the cattle and

[218]

horses were put in order again and they went on their way.

"They are all mine," she said, "on their way to the fair."

He chuckled in the darkness, "You handled them like a field marshal."

At a little before two o'clock she guided him into a long lane bordered by poplar trees, and after two or three minutes they came into a great paved open space before the farm. It was a kind of manor house, long and low and built by some one with a sense of balance and beauty. In the light from the motor he could see that at each corner of the house there were small round towers. They drove the car through an archway piercing the middle of the house, into a great shed, and she said: "We'd better go right to bed. We'll have to be up before daylight on our way, unless you're too lazy." All about them in the cool darkness was the smell he had once known so well—a smell of cows and hay and horses—the smell of a farmyard.

[219]

"No, I'd like it," he said.

Inside the house they walked through a great bare hall with a beautiful staircase at the far end, and into a small cool room where there were crocks of butter and pots of milk and cream on the shelves.

She took down some biscuits and said, "Would you like cider or milk?"

And then she took him up the stairs to a big room near to one of the towers. There was a little dressing-room in the tower itself, and in the room an enormous high bed with a great quilt stuffed with feathers. The bed was carved of walnut and had a canopy and there were a great carved wardrobe and three or four big chairs.

She took his hand. "Good night," she said. "I'll call you in the morning." Then she looked at him sharply. "You'll be all right."

She went out, and when he was left alone he stood for a time looking about him, aware of a profound sense of peace. This was a room in which people had been born, lived, made love, and died, for two hundred years. It went far back into the past and it would go on and on into the future. After he was dead, and Eliane and her children and her children's children, it would go on and on. There was peace in it. The world was no longer simply himself and his success. It had stopped whirring and jangling as it had done for sixteen years. There was something about this room which destroyed him, and that, he was aware, was what he desired. To this house he was only a stray visitor of no importance, for it would endure long after he himself and everything he had done was forgotten.

At last he undressed, climbed into the huge bed, and almost at once fell asleep.

They left before daylight, and a little after dawn they were in the great square of Rouen, where the cattle and the great horses and the sheep all stood packed together underneath the spires. There were rich Norman farmers there in their riding-breeches and high boots and tweed coats, so different from the farmers elsewhere in France. There was always the air of the English country squire about them. And there were droves of women and little boys, and the bargaining began almost at once.

He followed Eliane about as she bargained, aware that the men respected her not only as a good dealer, but as a handsome, high-colored woman as well. You could see that by the look in their eyes. They addressed her as Madame Harcourt and spoke of her as *"la veuve Harcourt."* Not one person at the fair had finer cattle and horses. She was a person of great importance, solid and rich and dignified, who occupied a great place in that world from which she would be missed when she died.

At noon she took him to a restaurant overlooking the square where Joan of Arc had been burned and there she ordered him an excellent lunch with Norman butter and fresh sole and a *galette de pommes.* The waiters all knew her. They addressed her by name, overlooking even the foreigners for her sake. It was as if during all these years since he had seen her last he had not lived at all, but only gone round and round in a kind of nightmare. Beside this life, his own had no substance, nor any meaning.

It was late in the afternoon when they returned, and he saw the *manoir* for the first time by daylight. The house was bigger than he had imagined, and on one side of it there was a pool of water which had once been part of the moat. On the side near the long avenue of trees there was a big garden, surrounded by a hedge and a wall, in which flowers and vegetables all grew together. But it was at the back of the house where the life of the whole big farm had its center. Here there was a great courtyard with a tank in the center, and an immense gateway through which the big carts drawn by white oxen or big Percherons came and went. On one side were the cowstable and dairy, and on the

[223]

other the stables where the horses were kept. Chickens and ducks ran about, and Guinea fowl clamored, and over the gateway there was a big square dove-cote murmurous with sound and alive all day long with fluttering pigeons. Beyond through the gateway one saw the expanse of paddocks and fields sloping down to the river and the water meadows where the sheep grazed and Pierre Harcourt had found his death one stormy night. Beyond lay the long low line of the beech forest where Eliane and the men of the place sometimes hunted the wild boars, that came on winter nights right into the garden itself to root up the rich earth.

All this he could see from the window. It was a whole world, and in the center of it stood the farmhouse and barns built long ago, like a fortress, about a square. Here was a whole world in which one might live and die without ever any necessity for leaving it.

When he came down from his room, three little boys came in, scrubbed and dressed in neat black suits. One of them was blond and the others were dark like Eliane. They came forward, one by one, and shook hands politely.

Eliane said, "This is a gentleman I knew during the war, before you were born." Then she named them in order.

"This is Pierre, and this Lucien, and this is Louis. Pierre is going to be like his father, a real Norman, big and blond like you."

Lucien, the second boy, said, politely: "Would you like to see our puppies? They're two weeks old." And Tom went out with the three of them to the end of the stables, where a sheep-dog bitch lay nursing her five puppies in the thick clean straw. Eliane remained behind to do her accounts.

He stayed for two days and then three and then for a week. The place was good for him, but most of all it was Eliane who did him good. He began slowly to see life as he had seen it

long ago, steadily and truly. It was impossible,
living in that atmosphere, talking day by day to
the busy Eliane, for it to have been otherwise.
After supper, when the boys had gone to bed,
he would go with her into the sitting-room and
then he would read and talk, while she did her
accounts or went through the papers from Paris
and the London *Times*, or talked to the steward
or the men who cared for the horses and the
cattle. Sometimes she would look at him suddenly, smiling and saying nothing, but he
thought she was trying to tell him how good
and rich a life this was and how right she had
been long ago.

And presently he began to have ideas again
and to take long walks in the beech forest,
thinking and planning. Once he said to her,
"You were right. This is good for me. I should
stay here forever."

But she only laughed, "No, not forever. Presently you'll begin to get restless and want to go.
I shall have to send you away in another week.

The boys' cousins are coming and there won't be room."

"I'll come back," he said, "if you'll let me. I'd like to stay, always."

"You can come back when you like. One more or less doesn't make much difference in a place like this. But staying always is something else. That won't do. It's too late now. Staying on would be giving up."

Then one night he had a letter from Jimmy Beaumont asking for a new play, and at the end, there was just a line which read: "Maisie has gone completely to pieces. She's in a sanatorium. I thought you'd want to know."

At first he thought of writing her, but abandoned the idea after reflection, because it seemed to him that it would only make everything worse. He had thought of her a great deal lately, mostly when he was away from the house and Eliane in the fields or in the forest, and now that he was less tired and ill, something of the old affection for her began to return. There was something about her, some quality of life, which made everything around her seem bright and more exciting. It was pitiable to think of her ill. Like himself, she was one of those who should never be ill. Indeed, he could not see her thus when he tried to imagine it. About whatever she did or said, there was a sense of vitality and excitement. He did not write her, but went for a long walk across the water meadows, and after supper that night when he and Eliane were sitting before the window, looking out across the garden, he told her the whole story, going back to the beginning, telling her about all the other women who had dulled his taste and made him hard. "At first," he said, "I was trying to find what we had known, and then I just became a *coureur* trying to amuse myself." He tried to tell it honestly, admitting his own faults and cynicism, and when he had finished she said, "So that was it?"

"No. It wasn't important. It was only part of the whole thing."

"It's more than you think," she said. "I think you'll discover that. Tell me more about her— just what was she like?"

He tried to tell her, and as he talked he came to understand that what Eliane said was true. He had never talked about Maisie thus to any- one. He did not know until now how pro- foundly he missed her, how exactly she fitted.

When he had finished, she put down her knit- ting and rose to go to bed. "It's a pity," she said. "You should have met her long ago and fallen in love with her instead of me."

That night when he went up to the room opening into the tower, he did a thing which he had never done before in his life. Before undressing he stood before the stained old mir- ror and regarded himself fixedly for a long time by the light of the oil-lamps, remaining quite still and staring into the reflection of his own eyes in an effort to discover what he was and why he found himself in so profound a muddle.

After a time it was as if he were hypnotized by his own image.

He thought: "It's true, what Sally and Maisie both said. I don't think about myself, at least not until lately. I've never thought about myself at all, nor what kind of person I am. I've never had time to study the subject. I've no idea what I am or what I'm like."

At first the gray eyes looked back at him cordially enough, and he thought: "That's a pleasant-enough look. I suppose I must look like that when I meet people for the first time—rather pleasant and frank and curious, almost inviting and certainly very friendly." And then as he continued to look at himself the face hardened a little and the gray eyes became faintly cynical and mocking and derisive—most of all derisive. Yes, he could see how that look would throw a woman like Sally into a fury. "And that, I suppose," he said to himself, "is the second stage, when people don't like me so much."

There was no vanity at the back of this

strange performance. He had seen his face in the mirror, casually, all his life, and he knew that he was neither deformed nor plain. Somehow there had never been any need for vanity, because everything had always gone so well and so easily. But now he wanted to go deeper and deeper, to explore far down inside himself; but presently the eyes became merely blank, a little sad, and somehow rather shallow, baffling him. He thought, "I can't be so bad as that."

Then after a moment he took up the hand mirror backed by ivory so old that it had long since turned brown, and for a time he regarded his profile from both sides. Then it was that he made a discovery. It was odd, but he found that he had the faces of three different men. Each side was different, and when they were brought together they made a third face, complicated, a little weary and a little dissipated. The jaws were square and the chin stubborn, the mouth was full and sensual and a little flabby with self-indulgence, and the eyes, when you looked

[231]

beyond the surface into their depths, were cold.

He did not like himself and he would rather have turned away than have gone on with the scrutiny, but the idea grew upon him that somehow out of this examination he might find some clue to the confusion and deadness of his mind and soul. He saw that if he were ever to regain his self-respect and his zest for life (and it was necessary if he were to go on living at all) he must change profoundly. It seemed to him, when he tried to remember how he had looked while shaving through all these years, that the face had already changed without his being aware of the difference. Certainly it was leaner and harder, narrower and sharper. The faint look of a bull which had always lingered in the neck and forehead—the look of a bull intent upon smashing his way through gates and fences and obstacles toward what he wanted— that look had given way to a new sharpness and fineness. It was this which made him feel that, after all, his suffering had been genuine and not merely born of whining and self-pity. And it was no longer a young face. Youth had gone out of it. It was not old or even middle-aged, but the last traces of that engaging look of youth which most lucky men have well into their thirties had gone from it. And this pleased him.

"Perhaps," he thought, "I've grown up. Perhaps I've got to be a man." Some men were like that, keeping a look of boyishness even into middle age. "Maybe," he thought, "I was a God-damned Peter Pan. I suppose most men who enjoy life are. Anyway, nice old ladies won't say to me any more: 'Oh, you can't be *the* Mr. Ashford. You're too young!'"

But what fascinated and frightened him was the thought of the three faces, so different and so contradictory, and after he had undressed and put out the lights and crawled into the high bed, he lay sleepless for hours, thinking about the strange phenomenon. There must be other

people who had two or three different faces, and
then it occurred to him that in the end perhaps
such people would destroy themselves simply by
the conflict of senses and personality. He wondered what he must do to pull the three faces
together into one which was strong and perhaps
even good; for now after years of mocking
gently at goodness, he divined that it could
bring with it great strength and even great
peace.

When Eliane had sent him away he would
have to begin all over again. He would have to
make decisions and straighten out all the tan-
gled threads and make a fresh start. He was
finished with the old house and garden forever, and he could not go back to Sally, who
had already found her way out without any help
from him. And as Eliane had said, he couldn't
stay forever here at the farm. Day after tomorrow he would have to leave, not cured, perhaps,
but at least with a new balance and strength
which he had found in her. And now she would

want to know what he was doing for all the rest of his life. He saw that she did not mean to lose him again as she had done once years ago. He dared not disappoint her a second time.

"She," he thought, "is strong and happy because she has only one face. She never had but one, even long ago when she was young. She always knew what she wanted and what life asked of her, and she has done her part without cheating. She'll go on doing it until the end."

And then, suddenly, he knew what it was. He had always been too greedy, wanting to stuff into him everything he found on the table of life. She had eaten well and like a gourmet. He was like a fat old man stuffing himself with wines and sauces and rich food until at last he dropped, destroyed, like the evil old man in Dickens' story, by a kind of spontaneous combustion. He had wanted everything from life— money and fame and success and love—and at the same time he had snatched at peace and simplicity and even solitude. He had wanted to be

Don Juan, and at the same time he had wanted to be a good husband and a good father. He had wanted, as he told Eliane, long ago, to know Paris and London and New York as he knew the farm in Illinois as a boy. He had wanted to know all the clever and successful people, and then suddenly he was fed up with them and hungered for the ancient still peace and obscurity of the old house and garden. He had wanted roots and tradition, and immediately he began to grow roots he became restless and bored and miserable because they held him to one place. And to have everything he had been ruthless and jostled and trampled others, even his wife and his own sons and Maisie, because that was the only way by which one could get everything.

The thought occurred to him that it was not altogether the fault of himself, but of the greedy, restless age in which he lived and of the greedy people to whom he belonged, always and forever. In the world there was very little peace and solitude left, and for Americans the only tradition was that there must be no tradition. They were forever being destroyed and reborn. If that were not true of them, then they were not good Americans. These people—his people—were nomads, from those who wandered across the vastness of their own country in broken-down Fords to those who moved restlessly from place to place in luxury over the whole face of the earth. When they grew roots, they were miserable. He wasn't the only American who had been frantically active all his life without ever having lived at all. He wasn't the only American who had funked it suddenly in the midst of life.

He thought: "That's it. I've got spiritual and moral indigestion. I must stop snatching at everything and find out what is good for me."

In the stillness of the night he rose and went over to the window in the little tower to look out. There was a new moon and the delicate virginal light painted the farm, and the courtyard with the tank of water in the middle, and the water meadows beyond, faintly with silver, and against the star-sprinkled sky the beech forest made a long thin line of black. Far off on the edge of the forest an owl kept up a faint, monotonous hooting that came through the night like the sound of a bell ringing underwater. In the stillness and peace he could hear an amorous pigeon ruffling its feathers and cooing in the dove-cote on the far side of the courtyard.

"Perhaps," he thought, "I am cured."

Suddenly he had had enough of this peace and was ready to go.

On his last day Eliane took him with her on the round she made once a month of the whole farm. They rode in a light cart drawn by a squat and shaggy pony—Eliane, himself, and Louis, the youngest of the boys. They rolled along deep lanes bordered by hedges and bumped through ditches and across fields, and once in the water meadows they became bogged so that all three of them had to descend and go on foot while

Tom led the pony. Eliane got down to go through flocks of sheep on foot, making certain of their welfare, and visited cows and calves and three great bulls which were kept apart in strong enclosures. She talked with farm laborers and their wives and entered the cottages, each with a well-kept garden before the door, to visit the children.

She sat very straight in the cart, guiding the fat pony, talking all the while, and now and then giving her small son a slap or a poke when he leaned too far over the side; and Tom, sitting beside her in the cart, so near that their bodies touched, saw her from a great distance, and still she seemed to him the most desirable woman he had ever known, not only for her charm and the power of her character, but also for that power which she had of making him— a stranger and a foreigner in this small world, a lover whom she had not seen for years—feel so simply at ease, as if he had always lived here. It might have been awful; with any other woman he had ever known it would very likely have been awful, but somehow she had the power of making it all seem right and simple and easy. He saw again that her strength came from the fact that she had only one face.

Once while they were crossing a wide pasture at the edge of the forest, the boy beside him suddenly cried out. "Look! Look! There's Paul's pony!" And Tom, looking up, saw a pony like the one that drew them, rear and snort and rush off among the mares and foals, and he said to Eliane, "Who's Paul?"

For the fraction of a second she was silent, and then in a low voice answered, quickly, "A friend of the boys'."

They had lunch in one of the distant cottages, and afterward drove home along the wide highroad between rows of beech trees. He kept thinking, "In the morning I shall have to go, and I would like to stay here forever."

As the evenings grew longer they had taken

to sitting outside on the flagged terrace beside the moat where they had a view of the avenue of trees leading down to the highroad. It was a quiet spot, and they would stay there, with their coffee and Calvados, until the last blue light had faded over the fields and the walled garden where the vegetables and flowers all grew together. Sometimes they read and sometimes they talked and sometimes they merely sat silent, feeling the long twilight, savoring it with all their senses, as they had done long ago in the little belvedere on the island.

On this last night she said, abruptly, "Have you made up your mind what you mean to do?"

"I don't know."

"You must go back to America. It's too late now for you to change."

"Yes."

"And go to work again."

"Yes."

While he sat talking he had been watching the highroad and the long lane leading down to it, lazily and without consciousness of what he was regarding, and presently he was aware that the omnibus had stopped at the end of the lane and that some one had gotten down and was now walking up the long avenue toward them. Who it was he had no way of knowing, but he saw that it was a man carrying a small bag. Eliane, sitting with her back to the lane and with the London *Times* open on her lap, talked on, unaware of his approach.

He heard her saying something about his being the kind of man who could not do without a woman in his life and who was the woman to be, and then it struck him that there was something familiar about the approaching figure, so familiar and yet so baffling that he forgot Eliane and did not even hear what she was saying. The figure was like that of some one he had known long ago in another life. The man was taller than most Frenchmen and walked with a shambling gait which wasn't at all French, for all the French were small and walked neatly, like cats, and this man walked like a woodsman, swinging out in his stride as if there were great distances to be covered. And then all at once, with a sensation of chill, he understood what the familiarity was—the fellow walked awkwardly like himself, as he seen himself walking in cinemas. It was an ugly gait. Eliane kept talking, but now he heard nothing whatever that she said. And then he saw that the figure was not that of a man, but of a big, awkward, over-grown boy. The boy came nearer and nearer, and Tom, fascinated, felt suddenly that he had gone mad, for it was himself that he saw approaching—himself when he was sixteen or seventeen, only this boy was dressed in tight, respectable, black French clothing instead of an ill-fitting suit which had come from a mail order house in Chicago.

Then Eliane stopped talking and, regarding him sharply, she said: "What's the matter?

[243]

Have you seen a ghost?" And he answered, "Yes, I think I have."

As she turned to look she gave a faint scream, the first sign he had ever seen her give of being startled or alarmed by anything. He heard her saying: "Paul! Where have you come from?"

The boy dropped the bag he was carrying, and Eliane rose and went toward him, and Tom saw that there was something between these two that was different in quality from the bond between her and the other children. He kissed her on both cheeks and then looked shyly at Tom and again Tom had a faint sense of madness. He was looking at himself. Tom Ashford at thirty-eight was regarding Tom Ashford at seventeen.

For a second Eliane was silent, but only for a second. Quietly she said: "This is Mr. Ashford, an American your grandfather and I used to know during the war, before you were born." She had recovered complete control of herself.

[244]

Her face had not even changed color. It was, Tom thought, afterward, nothing less than magnificent.

The boy held out his hand and Tom took it. It was a big, raw-boned hand which later on would be beautiful, but now was like the paw of a puppy—he had not grown up to it. "My hands!" thought Tom.

"How did you come home so soon?" Eliane asked him, and he told her that he was far ahead in his work, ahead of all the class, and so the fathers had allowed him to leave earlier. In his voice there was a fine edge of pride and of arrogance and of contempt for the others more stupid than himself. It was like the hands and the walk. There was an assurance in him that he would get what he wanted from the world, and one could see that he meant to have a great deal.

Eliane said, "Have you had supper?" and the boy said, "I ate a lunch I brought from school on the bus."

Then suddenly Eliane seemed to lose confidence in her power to keep control of the scene and she said: "Come into the house. I'll get you settled and bring you some coffee here." And she picked up the bag and led the boy with unnatural haste into the house.

When they were gone Tom thrust his hands against his head and pressed hard, as if by doing so he could bring himself back to reality, for in the whole scene he had found nothing real; it was like one of the dreams which had been troubling his sleep for months. He asked himself questions.

"Why had she never told him? If she had chosen to keep it a secret long ago, why had she not told him now when he met her again after so many years? How, with an illegitimate child, had she managed to marry and build for herself so firm a position in life?" She became more and more extraordinary to him. He understood suddenly the mysterious visits to Rouen and that sudden second of silent confusion when the

[246]

pony had galloped off across the fields and he had asked who Paul was.

Eliane and the boy were gone for a long time, so that he thought she must be explaining to him. While he waited he drank more and more Calvados, more out of anxiety than from desire. It was as if a bomb had been set off at the very center of his emotions.

The odd thing was that the sight of the boy, already almost a grown man, gave him more pleasure and excitement than the birth of his other two sons had ever done, and that in the moment of recognition he felt nearer to this boy than he had ever been to the other two, no matter how hard he tried. There was something wonderful in discovering suddenly a son who was nearly a grown man, to whom you could talk as a rational being, finding yourself in him; but there was something sad as well. For the first time in his life he felt old. He thought: "It's certainly time I settled down. My youth is finished." But at the same time the sight of the boy had brought his own boyhood nearer to him, so that it seemed only a little way off instead of misty and unreal. It seemed only the day before yesterday.

"I suppose that's American, too," he thought. "None of us is good at growing mellow or old. We never want to give up. And that, too, makes for confusion."

He had a feeling that the other two boys belonged really to Sally and Nanny and not to himself at all, but this boy was his—his and Eliane's—and he understood suddenly the timeless legend of the strength and beauty and charm of love children, and the story that such children were always cherished above others. This boy was made out of the beauty and passion of that first love between himself and Eliane. The others had been begot and conceived, indifferently, because they were a part of that vast scheme of things which he had demanded of life. They were needed to complete the picture of his own success. This other boy

[248]

he had loved at once because physically, at least, he was a recreation of himself far more than the others would ever be. They were finer, fine even to the edge of a faint decadence, not only in body, but in spirit as well. They would never have great, knuckled puppy hands. This boy was as close to the earth and to reality as he himself had been once long ago. "As I must have been," he thought, "when they found me there outside the gate." This boy was no stranger, like Peter and young Tom, with their expensive sort of life, their special diets and their toys, their advanced schools and expensive beaches and precocious knowledge of the world, learned second hand instead of by experience. He had been unable to save them, but Eliane had saved this one, out of that primitive wisdom and simplicity which was hers. This boy had all the chances for a good life, which he himself had had long ago. And then cynically he smiled and thought, "It is the old story, too, of Narcissus and the pool. That's what Sally and Maisie meant when

[249]

they called me a monster, only they hadn't the words to explain it."

Alone on the terrace under the trees he began to sing in a low voice out of sheer delight and excitement, and presently he saw that the discovery of this son had brought him very close once more to Eliane and to the old house and garden. Through Paul he had come back to them at last. The coming back, which in the midst of his illness he had divined as the only thing which could save him, was reality now. The spontaneous desire to sing, more true and profound than any reasoned process, was proof of it. He had found Eliane once more, and the peace and splendor of those weeks long ago in the old house; and Paul was the symbol that their love of long ago had not, after all, come to nothing. It was carried on and on in him and in his children and his children's children; nothing could ever destroy it. For he had discovered its living quality in the ardor with which Eliane had greeted the boy; and now he felt it within himself. For a little time it was like being truly one again, as they had been on that first night when he listened to the sounds of the old house until at last the footsteps came to his door and Eliane came into the room.

This was what she had meant by life being carried on.

When they came out of the house again it was dark and the hushed, mysterious sounds of the night had begun in the shadowy corners of the garden where the hedgehogs and night-ingales were stirring and on the edge of the forest the owl had begun once more striking its monotonous note, like the sound of a bell underwater. He watched them come down the steps, his heart beating with excitement, wondering whether she had told the boy anything. But when they were all three seated about the table with the Calvados and the fresh coffee, the boy gave no sign of knowing and he could not tell from the face of Eliane, because of the darkness. She poured a large cup of coffee for

Tom and said, cryptically, "Probably you'll need it."

The conversation was not easy at first, even in the darkness, what with the shyness of Paul and the sense of strain between himself and Eliane. Tom tried by questions to find out what it was that interested the boy most, and Eliane, divining what he was after, steered the boy with pride toward what it was Tom wanted to discover. The boy was shy at first, and then with little bursts of enthusiasm he got under way.

It was plants and animals. He was always experimenting with them. He had Guinea pigs and rabbits and a corner of the garden given over to beds of seedlings which he had crossed himself.

"In the morning," said Eliane, "you must show them to Mr. Ashford."

"If monsieur is interested," the boy answered, with a curious mixture of humbleness and pride.

"I can't think of anything that would interest me more."

Paul talked with modesty but with confidence, and when Tom asked him what it was he wanted most, he said, "A big farm like this where I can experiment and have the finest crops and cattle in the world."

He heard Eliane give a faint wicked chuckle and say, "He's ambitious and confident and intelligent like some others I know." She was enjoying herself.

Listening while the boy talked, Tom thought: "I should have been like that. I should have stayed on one track, and I might have had one face instead of three. There was a time . . ." But instead he had chosen the whole world.

Presently it became so dark that Tom could no longer see even the silhouette of the boy, but only hear his voice, warm and agreeable, coming across the table, speaking French, which seemed somehow all wrong, and at last Eliane said to him, "You'd better go up and get some sleep. Mr. Ashford is leaving tomorrow and we shall all have to get up early." And then Tom

[253]

divined that she meant to send him away, anyway.

The boy rose and again took Tom's hand and said good night, and once more Tom had the nostalgic sensation of shaking hands with his own youth.

They waited until the sound of his footsteps on the bare wood of the lovely staircase had died away, and then Tom said in French, "What did you tell him?"

"Nothing. You'd better speak English. Then if anyone is listening it won't matter what we say."

"Why did you never tell me?" he asked. "That would have been the natural thing to do."

In the darkness she was silent for a little time, and he knew that she was considering how she should explain it so that out of his different life with all its haste and storminess he would understand.

"It would have been the natural thing to do,"

she said, "but not the wise one. Suppose I told you long ago, when Paul was born, what good would it have done? It would have made you miserable and conscience-stricken. It would have wrecked all your ambitious plans. Being the way you were *then*, you'd have rushed away from New York and come over here and tried to marry me. It wouldn't have done any good. All three of us would have been in a mess, with defeat the end all around. Even if God had ever meant you to be a father and a husband, you were too young. You weren't much more of a man than Paul is now. In some ways less, with all your romanticism and refusal to accept things as they are. I knew it then. I know now how right I was."

She waited for him to speak, but he had nothing to say because she seemed, as she always did, unanswerable. Presently she said, "You mustn't think I had a hard time. It was easy enough. When my father died I had a little money, and when the house was sold I had some more. I went to England to friends I knew in London since I was a little girl, and I told them I was having a baby and that my husband was killed in the war. They were good friends, because they never gave any sign of not believing my story. They helped me, and Paul was born in their house. And when I came back to Paris it wasn't difficult. You see, most of my father's friends were painters or sculptors or philosophers, and they didn't think it very important whether people were married or not so long as they suited each other. Most of them were people of dignity and integrity who didn't need laws to make them behave decently. You see, my father only married my mother when I was born. They'd always meant to marry, but they never got round to it because it seemed less important to them than going into the village to buy the beefsteak for lunch. He married her on my account, because of inheritance laws and things like that."

Again she fell silent, and this time Tom's

curiosity spoke for him. "What about your husband?" he asked. "He wasn't an artist."

"Oh yes, he was!" she said, quickly. "People can be artists in many ways. He was an artist in how to live and that's the greatest art of all. It didn't matter that by accident he happened to be a farmer. He was a distant cousin of my mother's and he came to Paris to help me about complications over the inheritance. It was the first time we ever saw each other and he fell in love with me, just as you did, but in a different way. It wasn't a romantic love, but a terribly sure and right one. In the beginning I had pretended that I was a widow, but when he asked me to marry him and I wanted to do it, I couldn't deceive him, so I told him the whole story and promised him that I'd never see you or write to you again. That was what I meant to do, anyway, and you wouldn't be here now if he were still alive. He had a right to ask that of me. He asked me if I still loved you, and I answered him truthfully. I said that I did and

that I always would love the boy who fell off
the motorcycle at my gate, but that didn't matter because it was all finished and locked away
in my heart where it would never trouble him,
and anyway that boy probably didn't exist any
more except in my memory."

Listening to her, he began to have respect
and curiosity for this man she had married.
There was no feeling of jealousy, but rather one
of regret that he had never known and now
never would, because he was dead. Yet he was
aware of the presence of the man in the speech
and in the voice of Eliane whenever she spoke
of him. And he had seen it in her face again
and again—a light that was born of love and
respect for some one who was fine and clean
and noble.

"And everything," she was saying, "was on
my side. You see, he loved this farm, this land,
this forest. No one but his family had ever lived
here since before the time of William the Conqueror, and at thirty-eight he found himself

suddenly a widower with no children and no
one to inherit the place, because his first wife
was barren. He was sure of me. I had already
borne a child and I was strong and sure of myself. The need for sons goes very deep with
people who have lived always on the land.
There are still peasants in France who will not
marry a girl until she is pregnant, lest life and
nature play a trick on them and leave them without sons. Pierre wanted sons. He wanted this
place to go on as it had always done since the
Middle Ages, belonging to some one called
Harcourt who was a son of a son of a son. He
himself did not matter save as a link in the long
chain, and it was his responsibility not to break
it."

For a moment she was silent, and although
it was quite dark he knew that she was looking
at him sharply. Then slowly she said, "He knew
the most ancient and profound of truths, that
the individual exists only as a part of a great
scheme and that when the individual seeks to

become the whole scheme, there is only disaster and unhappiness. That's what my father preached, too—all his life—and made great sacrifices for it, too. Some day the world will have to understand that there is no room for ruthless ambitious people—if it's to go on at all."

Again she was silent and when she continued she said: "And so he married me in Paris and brought me and Paul back here, giving out that he had married a distant cousin who was a widow. No one seemed to doubt his word, and even if they had doubted it, it wouldn't have mattered, because he was a power in the countryside and, anyway, this farm is a whole world in itself and he was king of it. And after the first boy was born, he adopted Paul as his own son and then there were two more boys and he knew that the farm was safe with the Harcourts and the line would go on unbroken."

Her voice lowered suddenly, almost to a whisper: "I loved him. I love him still. He was a good man and a very wise man, and I was happy. Can you understand that there is a deep satisfaction out of making children in order that things may carry on—a deep, clean satisfaction quite as fine as making children out of passionate love for one another?"

Then she laughed lightly and said: "It was all very easy and simple. Perhaps I was lucky, but I had good sense, too, and strength. One has to know one's head and one's heart and not be a fool. But it was all very easy."

When she had finished he fell to wondering again what they were to do about the boy and himself. The moon had come up now, showing clear and thin and bright above the black line of forest, and by its faint light the body of Eliane, solid, black, a little plump, and quite serene took form again in the chair opposite him. Looking at the moon, he thought, "She was like that then—like a new moon." Nearly twenty years ago when he had opened his eyes to see her for the first time.

[261]

"Do you mean to take him from me?" she asked. "You might be able to do it. You could offer him so many shiny, glittering things."

"No. I shouldn't ever want to take him from you."

"You might do it without meaning to, the way you've done so many other things, without thinking about it, just because you had to have it. That's why I never told you. I was afraid. I thought you'd go away without ever knowing —and then he came home. Maybe I was wrong to take so much right to myself. Maybe I made a great mistake."

He was silent, weighing what she said, wondering, and she went on: "Maybe it was a mistake to have you come here at all. I asked you without thinking. I never thought you'd come to a dull place like this."

"No, that wasn't a mistake. You'll never know what a difference it has made." He could not describe to her the peace that had come into his heart nor how the desire to live, to see, to create had come back to him.

"I'll tell him if you like," she said. "Or you can tell him yourself. But the decision hasn't got anything to do with us. It's Paul we have to think about. You see, he doesn't suspect anything at all. I don't suppose he ever thinks of a father he never saw. Pierre was always his father." What she said hurt him, but she gave no sign of being conscious of it. She only went on talking quietly. "It's a bad age. He'll be eighteen his next birthday. It's a morbid age when a boy's whole life might be spoiled by a thing like that."

"You don't want him told," he said. "I think you're right. But it hurts. You see, I want to claim him. I'm proud of him. I want to help him, to give him everything—to spoil him . . ."

She interrupted him, "And there you are," she said, "the romantic again, thinking you are being generous and good because spoiling him would give you the greatest pleasure, and hoping that others will find a little pleasure, too, that has dropped by the wayside as you pass along your triumphant way."

It was astonishing how well she understood him and saw to the depths his weaknesses—his vanity, his romanticism, his delight in himself, which was neither egotism nor selfishness but more devastating because it was not simple. Unlike Maisie and Sally, she did not divine his faults vaguely and emotionally. She saw them clearly, and she had words to say what she meant.

"Later on," she was saying, "when he is older—when he's at a sensible age and maybe married, it wouldn't matter then. It would be better then for both of you."

"After he was married and having children of his own," thought Tom. "And I am a grandfather, at forty or forty-one." Aloud he said, "But hasn't he any suspicions when he looks at me? He's not a stupid boy."

He heard her laugh softly, "You, my dear

Tom, can remember what you looked like at seventeen, but how can he divine what he will look like at forty? Besides, I don't imagine he will look so much like Tom Ashford at forty as he does at seventeen. People's lives make their faces."

This time he knew that she meant to hurt him, and that in turn made him see how passionately she wanted to keep the boy and shelter him behind the bulwark of her own wisdom. She was trying to be fair—she was even trying in a way to atone for the fault of never having told him of Paul's existence, if indeed that was a fault, but in the depths of her nature she was fighting him now with any weapon she might find at hand.

"What is there I could do for him," he asked, "because whether we tell him or not, I want to help him."

Quickly and practically she said, "You could help to buy that farm he wants. Not now, but later when he marries and you've told him. You see, he won't inherit any of this. It all belongs to Pierre's boys."

The idea gave him a sudden swift pleasure. It would be like founding a race, a whole descent, a whole line like the Harcourts, which had gone on unbroken since before the time of William the Conqueror. Here in Normandy his blood would go on forever and ever. His other children were American; they would be attached to nothing. Even though they had children and grandchildren and great-grandchildren, there would be nothing permanent, because with them everything would be flux and change, restlessness and ambition. Perhaps in a thousand years there would be Ashford blood in this rich green country, as there was Harcourt blood now. And suddenly he saw clearly what she meant about the insignificance of the individual and the omnipotence of nature and continuity. It was fantastic that there should have been a vast war and so by accident and yet by the eternal design of Nature he and Eliane had been thrown together in that old garden. In the darkness he grinned. "Nature," he thought, "used us, and Eliane made the best of it with her wisdom."

He rose and bent down and kissed her cheek. "It's all right. I'll come back and tell him when you send for me." As he kissed her he discovered that she had been crying while she sat in the darkness talking to him in a calm level voice betraying nothing, and he remembered that she had said to him long ago, before he rode away on his motorcycle into the forest: "What happened to us was very wonderful. Some day you'll know how lucky we are."

Together they went at last into the house. The slender moon was high now in the sky, hanging above the distant beech forest, and its faint light fell through the big window at the turn of the old stairway. Here she stopped him and, taking hold of his coat, as if to prevent him from escaping, she said: "And you, my dear, you must go back to America. That's where

[267]

you belong. There isn't any place for you here. If you stay here you'll only rust and turn all mildewed and miserable. Go back and find that girl Maisie and pull her out of the pit into which she's fallen. That will give you something new to do—something you've never done before. Maybe you'll like it. Anyway, it'll be hard to do and once you didn't mind things that were difficult."

He looked away from her, out of the window toward the forest, but she still held him, saying: "No, I've not yet finished with you. Listen to me. You weren't meant to be a husband and a father. Your children are all right. You can trust me with Paul until he's settled in life. Your other children are all right, too. Your wife and that man James you told me about will look after them well. That man sounds like a good father." Again he saw her smiling at him. "You see, Nature makes use of men like you. You're good stock and you're intelligent and Nature meant you to be plagued by women and women to be plagued by you. It meant you to be just a breeding bull like those we saw in the field yesterday. They never worry about the calves they sire except when the calves grow up into bulls and get in their way. Believe me, I know about those things. That's the way life is, and there's no use trying to go against it. So don't try to be something you're not. Don't try to be everything. It'll only smash you up. Go back to Maisie. She's your kind."

In the morning she wakened him a little after dawn and they had breakfast together—Eliane and the four boys, with Paul sitting opposite to him. Outside in the great barnyard life had already begun. At the big tank in the center one of the farm boys was watering two great blond Percheron mares and a foal. The pigeons swarmed over the cobblestones, picking up the grains dropped from the carts which had come in late the night before. In the shadow of the shed a man in a black smock was yoking two big cream-colored oxen. There was a sense of well-being in the air which he had not known in many years, a kind of delight in being alive to greet the dawn.

The boy opposite him was less shy this morning. He talked with his small half-brothers and with Tom himself, quite naturally and without self-consciousness. The stiff black store clothes were gone, and instead of them he wore riding-breeches and a kind of short smock of blue denim, exactly the sort of smock Eliane had brought for himself long ago in the little village in the Valois. Watching him, the thought came to Tom that he had been fortunate beyond all hopes, for the boy opposite him was himself over again and he would lead another kind of life as different from his own as it was possible to be; and it occurred to him suddenly that this was what he had been wanting always—a son like this, in the image of himself. It was not that he was an egoist—it was only that he had been in love with himself always, as far back as he could remember. Don Juan must have been like that—always in love with himself—and so he never found satisfaction, for he had never really been in love with any woman. He had been searching always, interminably, restlessly, to find himself, and always he had failed.

After breakfast he went with Paul and his mother to see the rabbits and Guinea pigs and seedlings in the corner of the walled garden given over to the boy's experiments, and while Paul talked and explained all the curious things he had already achieved, Tom discovered in him another likeness, not to himself this time, but to Eliane's father—the little old mouse with bright eyes who had fought and fought and gone on fighting, sacrificing comfort, wealth, peace, and success for the sake of his fellow men. The boy was bending over a little bed of barley seedlings, and Eliane, plump and solid and dressed up in her best black dress, stood

[271]

on the opposite side, next to Tom. She was chuckling quietly, and when she caught Tom's eye, she said, "You see. He's like the old gentleman, too. He's carrying on what papa set out to do." Then aloud so that the boy could hear, she said, "You know, the radical parties are putting up a statue of papa in Paris and they've named a street for him. Wouldn't he laugh?"

When they had walked back to the house he discovered why Eliane was in her best clothes. "We're going as far as Rouen with you," she said, and turned to the boy. "Go and put on a coat, Paul. We'll go as far as Rouen with Mr. Ashford. It'll be a spree."

In the station where he left the two of them she drew him aside and said, "Now write to me about yourself, and when you want to come back let me know. Probably she wouldn't like it here. She'd probably be bored, being an actress."

"No," he said, "she wouldn't be bored." It was true. Maisie wouldn't be bored anywhere, because life had been too hard for her. Born on Ninth Avenue, she could fit into this life on a farm in Normandy. It was only pampered people who were ever bored.

"No," he repeated, as if talking to himself. "No. She wouldn't be bored. I'll bring her." It was odd that Maisie would one day find herself on a farm in Normandy, because there had been a war which dragged him all the way from Illinois to leave him unconscious with a broken head outside the gate of an old gentleman to whom they were erecting a statue in Paris because he had fought for the decency of the human race. No, life wasn't boring. It was . . . He searched for the word but could find no word which was magnificent enough. And suddenly he knew that he was cured.

The train pulled in and he saw them aboard it, waiting until it disappeared again out of the cavern of a station, with both of them waving to him lustily.

In Paris he looked up boats and then wrote a cable to Maisie which he addressed care of Jimmy Beaumont because he had no idea where she was. It read "Arriving fifteenth Ile de France Meet me at pier love Tom." When he read it through he tore it up and wrote another: "Arriving fifteenth Ile de France longing to see you everything all right please try to meet the boat I love you Tom."

And he sent another to Jimmy Beaumont. It read simply, "Okay Coming home." Jimmy, with his animal instinct and common sense and indestructible cigar, would understand. Funny, but in some ways Jimmy and Eliane were alike.

THE END